*Lisa,*

# Heist

## The Men of Law

*Happy reading.*

## CASEY CLIPPER

*thank you!*

What some are saying about Casey Clipper romance novels

*Heist*

"Casey has done it again! She has written a superb story! I know without a doubt this will be an awesome set of books! Heist has an unusual premise. Casey does a wonderful job of keeping the story grounded in reality. Heist is well-written, flows easily, has some twists, and grabbed my attention from the beginning. In case you haven't guessed by now, I loved Heist."

~Rebel & Angel's Book Reviews and Promos

*The Love Series*
*Silent Love*

"Silent Love is a book filled with angst, hope, and love. Casey Clipper delivers a novel that will have you swooning and snatching Sean up as a book boyfriend. The twists and turns Silent Love is filled with takes you on a roller coaster ride of emotions."

~Bottles & Books Reviews

*Unexpected Love*

"I can't believe how smoothly the words flow throughout this book. I loved all the characters. This story is also fast paced but you're not left wondering what's going on. I will definitely be reading more from Casey Clipper. I highly recommend this book."

~Bookaholic and More Blog

*Dangerous Love*

"Casey Clipper's third installment of the Love Series does not disappoint. I was pleasantly surprised to find that this story had a different spin to the traditional HEA story, which was perfect, considering Derk, the main character is anything but traditional. An unconventional love story with a non-traditional ending is what makes this a uniquely enjoyable read."

~Book Spots and Thoughts

*Taken Love*

"I have to say that I enjoyed this series from book one and with each book I grew to love it more and more. Smith in the prior books was more of a darker character but with Taken, Casey has brought him out to the readers like you would never expect."

~Jackie's Book Reviews

*Dedicated to all the loyal readers of romance, who embrace the traditional and non-traditional, because their love of a happily-ever-after knows no bounds and their acceptance of every author cannot be rivaled.*

# *Heist*

# CASEY CLIPPER

## 1

Detective Jason Campbell tried to recall if the law enforcement manual addressed panting like a dog in heat over a perp.

"This is by far the sexist thing I've ever watched," his partner, Dean Rooney said.

Nope. Nothing he could remember. No "Don't Drool Over Suspect 101" existed. He should pull out his old notebook from the training academy.

Jason hated to agree with his enthralled partner, but he couldn't help himself. It was hot as hell.

The surveillance video Jason and Dean, along with their chief and two other detectives, watched was a work of art. Well, a work of art in the illegal activity of thievery. A sense of déjà vu smacked Jason upside the head. How many times had this exact scene taken place over the past two years? Too many.

"No fingerprints, no close ups, no hair left behind, nothing," the chief growled in frustration.

Jason couldn't tear his eyes away from the television screen. The fluid movement of the perp's body, flawless. A smooth glide throughout the store as she ran her hand over the glass display cases, as if admiring the merchandise. Each gesture necessary and never a waste of energy, entirely aware of herself. Yes, the cat burglar was a woman. A woman with the body of a goddess. The form-fitted, black one-piece suit she wore accented every curve of her hourglass shape, as if it came straight from a movie set wardrobe department. More than likely, the clichéd getup purposely planned.

"Again, damn." Dean's sharp eyes zeroed in on the woman. His partner's usual reaction and commentary to each video they'd watched over the last couple years didn't disappoint.

Chief finally had enough and smacked Dean upside the head. "Knock it off. She's a criminal."

"Yeah, one I'd like to handcuff." Dean smiled wolfishly.

Jason mentally agreed. What he wouldn't give to handcuff that body to his bed. *Shit.* He needed to get a grip. Fantasizing about a thief only punctuated how long it'd been since he'd had a woman *in* his bed. *Damn it.* Stop it. Crim-in-al. An extremely talented criminal. He had no business daydreaming about her despite how long it'd been since he'd had the warmth of a woman in his arms.

"How much did she get away with?" Tyler O'Neill asked.

"Two fifty," Chief answered.

Dean whistled.

Two hundred fifty thousand dollars worth of diamonds. Man, the woman was upping her game. For just over two years, she managed to successfully break into every jewelry store in town and take what she wanted. At first she started off small, nabbing a thousand dollars worth of precious stones at a time, as if testing the waters. But over time, she increased her take with every heist. If they didn't catch her soon, they'd be forced to call in the FBI for help. No wonder Chief stalked around the unit cranky.

A fleeting thought crossed Jason's mind. Could she be practicing for something larger? That scenario made sense. Originally she hit the stores that had the least security to bypass. Each theft escalated to the next higher level of protection the businesses installed. Clearly the woman did her homework. Probably was an adrenaline junkie, as well.

"No women visiting the store days beforehand that might fit her physique?" Nick Butler asked.

Chief shook his head. "Nothing. The store only had a few visitors. A couple men browsing for engagement rings, an older couple interested in having a necklace appraised, and a teenage boy searching for a promise ring for his girlfriend."

"We can presume she's not working alone." Dean pointed to the screen where the burglar smashed into the case of flawless loose diamonds, scooping handfuls and shoving them into a black hip bag. "It would make sense. I don't know if she would be able to do this on her own. One of those men possibly cased the joint for her."

"You'd be surprised what a woman is capable of accomplishing on her own when she puts her mind to it," Chief murmured. Obviously a hidden meaning behind that remark that Jason and the guys weren't about to tackle. "The owner of the store gave me a list of names of all the customers over the past week. They'll be split among you to check out."

"Feds?" Tyler asked.

"Not yet. I've been contacted by a lead investigator of the FBI. They're fully aware of these jewelry store robberies. I'm trying to hold off as long as possible, but I don't see us having an extended period of time left. A few months at most. We need to step up and find her. I'll be forced to call them or they're just going to forcefully come in and take over without warning if this continues without an arrest. The last thing I want is them in our house," Chief answered.

"Shit," Jason said.

"Yeah, shit." Chief stormed out of the room.

Dean continued to drool over the screen and professed for the hundredth time, "Man, I think I'm in love."

Nick snickered while Tyler rolled his eyes.

"Down boy." Jason slapped his partner of seven years on the back.

Dean stopped the video, downloaded it to his laptop and sent the file to all of their email accounts. "Yeah right, as if that's possible."

Jason completely understood. This woman, with no visible facial features, but a body to die for, continued to star in his dreams and probably would until they caught her. How messed up did that make him?

## 2

Standing before her buyer, Hannah kept her guard up. She didn't trust the six men in the room. Their Sigs and Glocks conveniently out of the holsters clearly suggested the men gave her no credence, either.

"This is good," her buyer drawled. A receding hairline, slightly overweight, and a visible limp might frighten most women, but not Hannah. She'd been through tough situations with seedy characters before. At least these men didn't want her dead. Well, unless she tried to screw over their boss.

Carl, the man seated behind the mammoth oak desk, usually offered her reasonably fair payouts for her hard work. Only one time she argued the cash he offered for an excellent take. When she threatened to find someone else to purchase her "findings", he balked and gave her the cash that she desired. Since that transaction, their relationship flourished. All business, but fair business. He figured out quickly Hannah didn't bluff. She would research and easily find another buyer to take her stash off her hands.

"One fifty." He cocked an arrogant brow, blatantly goading her to argue. Not today.

Hannah nodded, aware that number was the best he'd offer. Two hundred fifty thousand worth of diamonds laid out on the desk before them. Carl's willingness to take the precious stones deserved the money he'd gross. If she managed to get busted, she wouldn't have the merchandise in hand. She refused to worry about getting caught. She had the best working with her to watch her back. But realistically, a chance that she might get busted always shadowed her. As long as she didn't have the diamonds, all remained kosher. That's what she told herself every night.

Carl smiled roguishly. "All right."

He heaved himself out of his chair and left the office. Probably hitting his hidden safe located somewhere in a backroom of the former home turned into some sort of headquarters. If the man meant to have the activities of the house to be obscured, he didn't do a good job of it. From the street, the wheeling and dealings of the home were clear. Expensive vehicles lined the lengthy driveway. Men roamed the finely landscaped lawn, guns, not exactly concealed, were visible from under their jackets. She could only imagine what happened in some of the rooms of this place. Especially on the second floor with the blacked out windows. But she'd never been harassed when she pulled up the driveway. She'd always been greeted as a business associate. Which she supposed she could adopt that title. The men even approached her car before she put the vehicle into park. They would open the door for her and lend her a hand out of the car. All very old school, gentlemanly mannerisms. Who knew those type of men still existed? More than likely it was due to the amount of wealth she brought into the fold. Honestly, she didn't care as long as they left her to her venture.

A few minutes later, Carl returned with a stack of bills, placed them on the edge of his desk, and slumped back down in his seat. "There you are."

"Thanks," she mumbled. Quickly, she scooped up the money, shoved the stack into her black tote, and left his office without another word spoken between them. Every meeting between them the same. Hannah preferred the arrangement. No reason for chit chat. Who cared about pleasantries? She just wanted her money.

Rushing out the door toward her BMW Z4 Roadster, she jumped into her convertible and peeled out of the driveway over one hundred grand richer. And now free from the syndicate. At least temporarily. After her last take, not only had she paid off her mother's debts, she ended her father's gambling indiscretions as well. She managed to ward off another surprise visit from oversized collectors wanting the money owed by her *stellar* parents. It might also have helped that she couldn't be found at the moment. Changing her name, appearance, and the state she resided helped to avoid those unwelcome ambush visits on her doorstep. She dealt on a strictly cash basis for all bills, leaving as little crumbs for anyone to follow as possible. The people her parents owed the money received an unidentifiable package with a little note whose payment that cash went toward. This cash stash would be her nest egg.

Twenty minutes later, after a mind clearing drive and allowing the wind to blow through her fiery red hair on the warm, last day of summer, Hannah pulled around back of a ratty apartment building. After raising the roof on her beloved car and locking up, she dashed inside and took the steps two at a time to the second floor. The building—rundown, screaming children from behind apartment doors, numbers falling off doors, chipped, lead-ridden paint—vividly reminded her of her childhood living conditions. A cold shudder snaked down her spine.

Knocking on apartment B, she heard the television go mute.

"Who's there?" Roy barked from the other side of the door.

"Damn it, Roy, it's me." Even though earlier she assured him she would be by around this time, and his only other company consisted of the UPS delivery driver, he still allowed his neurosis to control him.

The apartment door swung open, Roy reached out, grabbed Hannah's hand and yanked her inside his place, locking the dead bolt behind them.

She rolled her eyes. "Paranoid much?"

He wagged a long, thin finger at her. "You're not suspicious enough."

She shrugged. "What's the worst that can happen? I go to jail. Free cable and three daily meals and I'll get the hell away from *Mommy* and *Daddy*."

Sympathy promptly crossed over Roy's features. He was the only person in her life who knew her entire sordid past. Hannah despised those expressions from him or anyone else. She could still envision her parents' neighbors' faces when the seedy men knocked on the door while she played on the dilapidated swing set in the courtyard of the apartment complex they lived. At the time she hadn't known what those pity glances meant.

"Don't." She drilled him with a glaring look. She loathed Roy's empathy.

"Sorry," Roy mumbled. Motioning toward his living room, Roy invited her inside.

Hannah leisurely followed her good friend into the only room in his apartment where he performed his brilliant work. Bookshelves lined the walls, filled with computer and electrical equipment, books, and tools that resembled an auto parts store. His workbench sat front and center, facing the sixty inch television, where he constantly focused—tuned into an episode of NCIS, as usual. Roy could rattle off realistic and fabricated for TV details of every episode, even quoting specific lines.

She pulled out fifty thousand dollars and slapped it onto his bench table. "Thanks."

"Did it work?" His anxious eyes went wide with anticipation.

"It did." She grinned wryly and winked. "Brilliantly."

"Yes," he hissed.

Roy managed to create a device that interfered with the security cameras that tried to zero in on her during the heists. She had no clue how the contraption actually worked, something about frequency and currents, or whatever. But as long it kept the cameras at a distance recording, all was good. She loved the idea of teasing law enforcement with a far off recording, unable to get much off her description due to the cameras wouldn't zoom in. She couldn't deny the rush she got with each heist, that knowledge wedged in the back of her mind.

"Those little lights went off as soon as I turned it on," she said.

Roy's expression was pure elation. "How distressing for the police."

She giggled along with him, relishing in the fact she kept the cops at bay. She could envision a room filled with overweight, egotistical men cursing that a five foot two inch woman ran roughshod over them.

"You do know the feds will get involved eventually, right?" he warned. "I hacked into the police files. It's only a matter of time before the department has to call them in. In fact, I'm surprised the local police haven't. You've been a menace to them, dragging these detectives along for far too long. The feds are actively involved in the other areas you've hit."

"Yeah," she answered. "I'm going to have to start spacing out the heists and be more thorough in which shops I choose from here on out."

Roy stared her down, as if she was an electronic device he needed to figure out how it worked. "You can quit. You have that debt paid off. They won't come after you any more."

"Not true. They won't return until the next time. And there is always a next time." Avoiding eye contact, Hannah turned away from Roy, dressed in his normal attire of what she dubbed his Heff pajamas. She went to the window to stare out at the bright day. Two young boys darted down the street below, chasing a black Lab. Idolizing their carefree spirit, watching them laugh together, a stab of yearning threatened to surface. She'd been denied that youthful abandon as a child.

She resolutely suffocated the unacceptable reaction. Hannah felt secure. Never in her life had she experienced the luxury of financial freedom. She had plenty of money stashed away to buy her out of any issues. If she hit another store or two, a couple major scores, she'd be set for life.

But a return of the men her parents consistently owed money always hindered her from personal liberty. She could never say she was totally free and clear from their drug and gambling debts. Deep down she knew that as long as she continued to pay, they'd continue to borrow, and the men who gave the money would continue to pay out. Because they weren't losing cash. Just a little time and effort to hunt her down. Other than that, they got their money with significantly outrageous interest added onto the total. They couldn't get blood from a rock–her parents–but they knew Hannah didn't favor broken bones. Win for them. Not so much for her. But she did what she had to in order to prevent further physical harm, possibly an early grave, or be dragged back to living in the slums of this world. She didn't have a choice. She had no skills, no college degree or trade school education. Working at a department store or fast food restaurant wouldn't give her crap. Robbing banks and dealing drugs risked too much. But jewelry stores had insurance for these types of losses. They'd have no problem replacing their stock and she'd grab quick money from selling the product on the street. No one got hurt and she stayed alive with all appendages intact.

"You're skinny." Roy's inflection came across as accusation.

Flinging her head back, Hannah laughed. "Only you could make that sound like I committed a crime."

"What are you doing to lose more weight that you certainly don't need to?"

"I'm working out harder." She gave him a satisfied smile. "I've increased my weights and cardio. I've been working with the trainer at the gym, gaining strength. Some of the entrances and exits of the stores require too much upper body strength that I don't have. Well, *didn't* have. I'm working on that flaw every day." She squared her shoulders proudly.

When Hannah first went on the move, she'd been a plump thing. Forty pounds overweight didn't help fight off the goons sent after her parents in New York, when she'd been caught in the crossfire. After the loan sharks released her to find their money, she vowed never to allow that occurrence to happen again. She worked her ass off, running and dieting to lose the extra poundage. She went to local libraries where she would spend hours reading weight loss books on how to help rapidly shed the pounds. When she lost thirty, she turned her workouts into muscle training. Now she weighed one hundred and ten pounds and had freakish strength. Except when she glanced down, she still couldn't see her feet past her double D chest, the one area that hadn't shrunk. Who knew how she managed to accomplish that feat?

"Just so you're not starving yourself." His mouth set in a stubborn flat line.

"Nope, still love spaghetti." She winked.

Roy cracked a smile, his hazel eyes lighting up. He was her best friend. Her only friend, and vice versa. Hannah understood him and didn't judge. It didn't matter that he feared people and the outside world, causing him to become a recluse. His obsession with law enforcement and investigative shows didn't bother her. She found his ramblings about technology endearing. Okay, she poked fun at him, but only lightly, taking care not to ruffle his feathers too much. Roy was the sibling she never had. As long as she stayed a fixture in his life, they both accepted the rare, odd bond they had together and each other's quirks.

"Hungry?" she asked.

"Yep." His eyes flashed and he visibly cringed.

Her hackles went up. Fucking Roy.

"Any food in that fridge or cupboard?" She raised a censorious eyebrow, aware of the answer.

"Nope," he whispered.

She cursed under her breath. "Fine, I'll order a pizza and go to the grocery store. Make a list. Damn it, Roy. You have to call me when you need food or anything else. You know I'll go to the store for you. Quit thinking you're imposing on me. What else do I have going on besides trips to the gym and casing jewelry stores? Don't go hungry out of embarrassment."

"Thank you." He focused on the worn tan carpet.

Roy didn't live near a grocery store or pharmacy that delivered. When his cupboards went bare, he remained screwed until Hannah realized his pantry was empty. Thank goodness she bought him toilet paper in bulk.

She pushed off the window sill and lifted his chin to peer into his eyes. "Hey, don't feel ashamed. I just want you to call me when you need something. Please. I'm more than happy to get you whatever you need. I don't want you to presume you're a burden. Ever. You take care of me and this is one way I can take care of you."

Roy nodded, his face beet red. Her heart ached for him and his debilitating fear. She didn't quite understand it, but after some research, she sympathized that his mindset wasn't an act. Roy was truly petrified of the world outside his apartment door. If she gave him this small amount of peace, not having to worry about when his next meal might be, she'd do whatever necessary to take the time to shop for him.

What he did before she accidentally stumbled over him, immobilized in the chain store four years ago, she didn't know. How she got him to move to his current residence, closer to her place, showed the depth of their friendship. He only agreed when she volunteered to do all the moving, assuring him he had nothing to be concerned about, and gave him an extra dose of Xanax for his physical move.

Hannah stood on her tip toes and kissed his cheek.

"Go make your list while I call the pizza place," she said.

Roy dutifully grabbed a pad and pen and went to the kitchen. She watched him with a sadness and unease that if anything happened to her, he may end up alone without anyone to care for him, cementing a bleak future.

What a long ass day. Tired, pissy, and hungry, Jason found himself growling as he pushed a grocery cart around the store to pick up some sort of nourishment. Why the hell did he put off shopping for so damn long? He really needed to hire a personal shopper or ask his mom to help out. No food stock in his house currently bit him in the ass. Especially when his body wanted to collapse from exhaustion at any moment.

Jason trudged down the aisles and straight to the prepared food section. He snatched a call number and waited. While he stood, propping himself on his cart, his eyes scanned his surroundings, a habit from his years of service in the US Marines and as a patrol officer.

"Hey, big fella, would you mind moving so I can get to the potato salad?"

Startled, Jason straightened upright, and hovered over a tiny elderly lady looking up at him expectantly. Where the hell did she come from? So much for awareness. Shit.

"Sorry, ma'am." He moved his six foot three inch frame out of her way.

"Thanks, honey." She patted his arm in a grandmotherly fashion.

A droned voice called his number.

Jason approached the counter and placed his order. Thank goodness for the prepared fried chicken, macaroni and cheese, green beans, corn on the cob, and ribs that would relieve him of cooking this evening and immediately fill his angry stomach.

After receiving his order, he rushed around the store grabbing whatever caught his eye. Grocery shopping did not make the list of his favorite pastimes. Milk. Crap, he by-passed that section. Without a glance behind him, he whipped his cart around crashing into another with a loud clatter.

"Shit, sorry." He glanced up and his heart just about stopped. A goddess stood before him. Flaming red hair, large dark blue—almost black—eyes, and flawless fair skin, like precious porcelain. Except the woman before him didn't exude dainty. She was pissed. Those eyes shot daggers his direction.

"Really?" she snapped.

"I apologize."

Her perfectly manicured eyebrow arched high on her forehead. Well, if she was going to be a bitch he could be an asshole.

"I said I was sorry. In most polite cultures, people accept an apology and move on," Jason snarled.

She snorted, the sound obnoxious, sarcastic, and humorous. "In most polite cultures, people glance around their environment to make certain they don't knock someone over. What if I had been a little old lady? I could have ended up on the floor."

"You certainly aren't a little old lady and I have a suspicion, difficult to knock down." Even he heard the disdain drip from of his tone. Man, he didn't have time or energy for this crap. This woman irritated him. "Like now, you won't fucking move."

In retaliation, with an impressive strong push, she rammed her buggy into his with so much force she knocked the entire thing on its side. Jason stood there, stunned. She breezed past him with her full cart, head held high.

"There. I moved," she said, all too sweetly. With a flip of her hair, she rounded the corner out of sight.

Normally, he'd have fallen to her feet over her feistiness and the sway of her hourglass hips, but his fatigue skewed his appreciation, finding it annoying as hell. Technically, he could arrest her for disorderly conduct. But that would involve time and paperwork. To hell with that.

Sluggishly, he bent down and picked up his scattered groceries. At least his hot food stayed intact in the cartons. She had a point, though. He should have glanced behind him before he whipped his cart around. But was her overreaction necessary? God help the man in her life.

Jason certainly didn't feel well rested, but his alarm argued with his body that it was time to rise and shine. Physically and mentally, he was spent from long hours and endless days of reviewing tapes and footwork on their jewelry thief. It also didn't help that his sleep had been riddled with images of a spirited redhead pinned underneath him while he drove his body into hers. He woke with the hardest erection he'd had in a very long time.

Moments like this made him quite aware of his loneliness. He hastily reminded himself of what his law enforcement brothers had gone through in the past with relationships. He didn't need to deal with that type of hassle or heartache. Dean and Nick's marriage history alone, cautioned him to date but never fully commit. His job needed him clear-headed, not worried about his home life. His tiredness currently put his work in an endless blurry haze, which didn't bode well either for any tied-up intimacy consideration.

Allowing the hot water from the shower to stream down his tense body and relax his tight muscles, Jason palmed himself to an unsatisfactory orgasm. Talk about useless. Why had he bothered? He picked up a bottle of body wash and started to cleanse himself, his mind running a million different directions at once. For some odd reason, the shower always brought on his best thinking. Where did it go to this morning? The jewelry burglar.

This case wore on him and the rest of the team. They weren't any closer to catching her than when she first appeared a couple years ago. Dean was right. There was no possible way she worked alone. Which begged the question, how many people were in on the heists with her? Or were they working for her? Had to be with her. The mastermind always made themselves hands-on in cases like these. He gave her credit for her brilliancy. She managed to elude them. But all they needed was that one break. That one lucky tidbit to lead them straight to her. A fingerprint, hair, DNA, a witness or close up. Hell, a picture of a tattoo or scar would give them something minute to go off of. But whatever technology she used to encrypt the video feed and prevent their guys from retrieving any potentially identifying information from the cameras was far more advanced than what they could decipher. Or had access to without bringing in a task force or the feds. How large was this woman's operation?

After he scrubbed and shampooed, Jason climbed out of the shower and dressed for another shift. He contemplated placing a request for a week vacation. His last period of time off other than a weekend? Over three years ago. Well before the sexy jewelry thief made her first appearance in their area. He could use vacationing with his parents as an excuse for a couple weeks off. His mom would be over the moon if he made that happen.

Dressed in his suit, Jason rushed to the kitchen to pour his freshly percolated coffee into his travel mug and sprinted out the door. He didn't have to carpool with Dean today, which regularly made them a half an hour late. That man and his morning pastry shop stop always turned into a gab fest with the young women behind the counter.

When Jason pulled his car into his assigned spot at the precinct and climbed out of the sedan, his body cramped, tight and achy. So much for that hot shower. When was the last time he visited the gym? Weeks, and apparently his muscles weren't happy about the lack of attention. This damn case kept him from his normal routine. And from keeping track of his life outside of the job. If such a thing existed.

He made his way into the building and to his desk. Before his ass hit the chair, the chief poked his head out of his office. "Campbell, meeting."

Two words that were like nails on a chalkboard to him before he managed some sort of breakfast.

Jason shuffled toward the brainstorming room, where he swore he just left. Chief, Tyler, and Nick already waited. Tossing himself into a chair, he focused on the white board. Pictures of their perp taped to the board from all available angles with dates, times, and locations in black marker suggested someone had been up well into the night. Probably Chief, who had no one to go home to in the evenings, either. They really were a pathetic group of single-status detectives.

"I have an idea of where our girl's next possible target might be." Chief threw out with no preamble. Typical. Chief may have three years in age on him, but the man held wisdom beyond his thirty-seven years.

"What's that boss?" Dean asked, all smiles, sauntering into the room. Must have picked up a fling last night. No matter how late or how many hours they worked, Dean always contained enough energy for a good piece of ass. His words. And he managed to get a lot of it.

At the center of the board, Chief pointed at a picture of a jewelry store. "McIntyre's."

Silence, except for a couple shifts in squeaky chairs, descended upon the room. They were fully aware of the ramifications if McIntyre's became a victim of the thief. A premier jewelry store in the entire state of Pennsylvania that happened to be located in their suburban town. The family owned business didn't just carry millions of dollars in diamonds, their price ranged into the billions. Including pieces worn by British royalty and the Hollywood elite. Their jewelry had its own security nearby as the stars that dripped with the precious gems walked the red carpet. If their burglar managed to steal from McIntyre's, no store would be safe. McIntyre's prided themselves on the latest and greatest in security. They had to in order to protect their assets.

"Why do you think there?" Nick asked, his skepticism evident.

"First, in the past two years she's managed to hit every store in our township, except for one. Over the past few weeks, I've done some deep research and talked to some acquaintances in nearby precincts and task force members who happened to have knowledge in this crime spree. Before our area, numerous jewelry store heists took place throughout Western Pennsylvania. She spread out those robberies. Jewelry store break-ins that go as far north as Erie have spanned ten years. All remain unsolved and all have her MO. No large amounts of merchandise taken, minimal security, nearby highway access. She steals and leaves. For some reason she's settled in our town and there's only one untouched store. McIntyre's is it." He pointed to the picture of the flashy building located in the heart of the downtown shopping district.

"I can't fathom she'll move on until she hits the mother load at McIntyre's," Chief added adamantly. "Campbell and Rooney, you two make contact with the store and see if they're willing to help us catch this woman."

"Use the store as bait?" Tyler about screeched. If anyone wouldn't see this plan as viable it would be Tyler. A by-the-book, knows all the rules, doesn't walk outside the lines, detective rookie. Someone needed to show him there was more to life than studying the detective manual every night. Hell, the kid needed to get laid, relax him. Didn't he have a girlfriend?

"I like it." Dean gave a reptilian smile.

"You only like it in the hopes of being able to catch and handcuff her," Tyler spat, completely offended.

"And?"

Jason snorted through his sip of coffee.

"And that goes against procedure. She needs to be brought in for questioning and have the book thrown at her." Tyler crossed his arms over his chest, reminding Jason of a petulant teen.

Banging his fist off the table, Chief was not a fan of Dean's witty banter and Tyler's stick up his ass. "Enough! Focus."

Jason slanted Dean a side glance. His partner grinned his direction.

"You two go there and feel out the store, see what kind of help you can get. They should be willing, although they might not like the attention and may claim that they can handle this woman on their own. I don't think for one minute we should underestimate her. She can't be working alone. We haven't seen any evidence otherwise, but that doesn't mean that each place she's broken into hasn't had perimeter points of help." Chief tapped the top picture, a still from the video they watched yesterday. Her shapely form taunting the men in the room. "She's no fool and she's not playing games. We need to catch her before something goes wrong or someone gets hurt."

With that, they were dismissed.

Jason stood with Dean. Before they left to visit the jewelry store, they both refreshed their coffee mugs. Hopefully Chief was wrong and the McIntyre family would willingly cooperate. He hated to think a store might take matters into their own hands. That would be dangerous for everyone involved.

Hannah savored the warm sun shining bright while a breeze kept her cool enough to sit on the outside deck of the coffee shop and enjoy her novel. She loved to read. She favored romance, especially motorcycle clubs and erotica. Currently, she read through a series about former military special ops men who worked in Texas and lived the BDSM lifestyle. Fun.

She picked up her coffee and took a long sip, her gaze swinging to the store across the street. McIntyre's. She couldn't decide if she wanted to hit the "big one". Talk about retiring at the young age of twenty-nine. Scoring on that building had the potential to run into the millions of dollars—as long as she stayed disciplined and away from the designer jewelry. If she elected to go through with this one, Hannah needed to stick with the loose pieces of diamonds and jewels that could easily be sold on the street. If she took the recognizable designs, she'd have to find another buyer. Carl would refuse to take them off her hands. Plus, those specific designer pieces could quickly lead back to her.

She went back to her novel. She had some time to decide but not enough to dawdle. It took a couple months of plotting with Roy to pull off one of her heists. No doubt McIntyre's would take longer to map out and research.

As she continued to read, her mind wandered and she caught herself peeking at the front door of the establishment that held so much potential. All the work she'd done over the years to not get caught told her to choose a different store. One in another town. One not so close to her home, easy access to the parkway, and doesn't have state-of-the-art security, as well as twenty-four seven armed guards. But to have the financial security to ward off another visit from her parents' gambling and drug thugs held too much weight over her.

Hannah gnawed on her bottom lip, pushing down the overwhelming temptation. She needed to stay in control and focused. Another glance to her left and an unmarked police car pulled up in front of the store. Interesting.

Two men dressed in dark gray suits climbed out, the driver vaguely familiar to her.

A young male barista approached, standing in her line of sight. "Are you doing okay?"

"I'm good, thanks." She looked up through her dark sunglasses, giving off that unspoken aura to leave her alone. He swiftly scooted away to bother another customer.

Hannah lounged back in her seat and picked up her e-reader. Her mood didn't favor getting dolled up today. A pair of VS yoga pants, an oversized T-shirt, and slippers went well with her mood.

As she continued to read her novel, occasionally peeping across the street, she observed the changing of the guards at the front door and a couple employees meander into work. The other day, she noted that the store brought their staff in on stacked shifts. She picked up her phone and typed in a memo of the date, day, and time of the change. When she returned home, she'd jot the information down in her notepad and delete the notation on her phone. Details.

She kept her details under severe scrutiny. If she ever got caught, the police would find nothing on her phone or laptop. Roy did all the leg work from his computer, kept all tidbits organized, and he knew how to dump the information. Well, he knew how to get rid of a hard drive, which was the only way to really hide any unlawful research information. As for her paper notes, nothing a lit match couldn't take care of.

She pushed her thick long hair off her shoulders. Her phone dinged and she picked it up to see Roy emailed her. *Stop by today, have some new items for you.*

Hannah grinned. A boy and his toys.

Suddenly, the chair across from her scraped the wood floor and a large body plopped down in the seat. Annoyed, her gaze swung up and she lost her breath.

## 6

Jason and Dean weren't in the jewelry store fifteen short minutes before the owners denied their willingness to cooperate with their investigation. They were convinced their own security was more than adequate and didn't want attention brought to the business by the local police department's presence. Expressed not so kindly by the owners. No matter how Jason tried to explain the situation, the owners remained resolute.

As Jason and Dean left the jewelry store, frustrated, Jason was about to climb into his car when he spotted her. The woman who managed to run roughshod over him last night.

Without warning his partner, he abandoned Dean and went straight to the coffee shop and sat himself down across from her. Her head snapped up and he saw her eyes widen behind those designer sunglasses.

"Hello," he said, pleased by her startled reaction.

A young female barista approached. "Can I get you something?"

"Yes, large black coffee to go. She's buying." He pointed to the ginger.

She scoffed, an adorable sound. "You wish."

"You are. You owe me for last night."

"Last night? Honey, I was home alone last night. Sorry, you must be thinking of someone else." She shoved her reading device into a cover, sat up straight and pushed her sunglasses up on top of her head.

For a second, he thought she was serious, until he realized she purposely played coy. The mirth in her dark blue eyes gave her away. "Nice. You know what

I'm talking about. I had to pick my groceries up off the store floor as a result of your cute temper."

"Cute?" she said, offended. "Cute?" She tested the word.

Dean appeared, sliding too gracefully for a man into the seat next to her. "Why, hello."

His redhead rolled her eyes. "Oh for God's sake. Do you two have nothing better to do? Isn't there a speeder or someone that needs a ticket?"

Jason blanched. "How did you know we're officers?"

She outright laughed at him. "Your flashing your badge."

She pointed to his waistband. He glanced down at his waist and sure enough, his jacket was open with his glossy badge glimmering her direction.

She stood, grabbed her coffee, purse and reading device. "I'm not buying you coffee. Clearly you need to work on your game." She gave Dean a calculated once over. "And he needs to lay off his. Good lord, you two need help."

With that, she away walked briskly, her hips swaying under those far from sexy pants. Except on her, they worked well.

Dean whistled. "I think I'm in love."

Yeah, his partner wasn't the only one.

## 7

Hannah held her breath until she pulled away from the coffee shop. Somehow she managed to keep her cool while being confronted by a *detective*. Law fucking enforcement. That man could have pressed charges against her the night before. Man, she needed to check her temper. Yet she couldn't deny that being placed in a pair of cuffs by that yummy hunk of a stud would be somewhat of a turn on. That disarming thought slammed home how long it'd been since she welcomed the hot embrace of a man.

She whipped down the road, her hair flailing around her. At a red light, her mind reeled at the possibility that last night she could have ended up in jail. Would they have figured out what extracurricular activities she favored? Who would she call if she got arrested? Roy? She couldn't get him to step into the hallway of his apartment building let alone post bail. Her parents were lost causes. Carl? No. There was absolutely no contact allowed with the man unless she had something for him to buy. He made that very clear at their first meeting. And getting in touch with him usually took a couple days. He wasn't an immediate return-call man.

Suddenly an idea hit her. She sat up, her back going ramrod straight. A cop. No, a detective. That man with the colossal muscular frame, which strained against the gray suit he wore, and who stood over six feet tall, visited McIntyre's for a reason.

Why? Were the police on to her?

No, she couldn't be a suspect. He wouldn't have approached her. Or would he? No. If he chose to make contact, it would most certainly be undercover.

Was he picking up an engagement ring?

No. He wouldn't sit his big body into the seat across from her and clearly flirt. Well, his pitiful version of flirting.

She drummed her fingers on the steering wheel, ideas developing. Perhaps having someone close to her, who may think to confide in her about cases on the docket, might benefit her greatly.

A loud horn honked, shaking her from her racing thoughts.

Hannah took off toward Roy's apartment. Time to get an opinion on a possible tactic that might help her find out what the police knew and didn't know, and why two officers stopped at the premier jewelry store in the state.

***

"You want to do what?" Roy gave her a tremendous frown.

Hannah studied his reaction. "I think it's a good idea."

"You do realize that trying to get close to a cop is like holding a fresh piece of raw meat in front of a shark, right? Have you lost your mind?" He paced around his small living room, raking his hand through his long, greasy black hair. No matter how many times Roy washed those thick tresses, he never appeared as if he showered.

"I won't get close to him. Only enough for a couple dates. We can chat, cover a few topics while getting to know each other. Then oops, in passing, he mentions the heists, which have also been touched upon in the news. He won't think he's giving me any information I don't already know." She crossed her left leg over her right as she leaned back into the burgundy plush sofa cushions. "I innocently probe a bit and, bam, find out what they know. I'm lucky to have bumped in to him."

Roy stopped and faced her, his eyes narrowing. "You give yourself too much credit. You're not cagey enough to try and work this. And law enforcement don't possess confession skills. They don't spill their guts to their family like they're talking about last night's football game. This isn't your type of scheme. You have a conscience. You can't manipulate people. Again, have you lost your mind? Did you bump your skull? Have you eaten some bad chicken?"

She tilted her head. "Bad chicken can affect someone's decision making?"

"You know what I mean!" He pulled at his shirt sleeves, a nervous habit. "Goddamn it, Hannah. Think. This won't work and you could end up in jail."

She stood and approached her only friend. She was causing him stress. Something he didn't need with his already high anxiety level. She placed her hands on his shoulders. "I understand what you're saying. Believe me, I do. But I want to give this a try. There's a reason the cops were at McIntyre's and I want to know why."

"You shouldn't even be focusing on that place. You should choose a different store. McIntyre's will get you killed." His expression became stricken and terrified. "They have armed guards."

"I'll be fine."

"No you won't."

"Roy, as long as I have you helping me, I'll be fine."

"And what if I don't agree to help you?" He may as well have stomped his foot and pouted.

"I guess I'll have to walk away." She hoped Roy wouldn't withhold his vast computer knowledge and hacking capabilities to thwart her plan.

"I won't help you." He turned from her and slumped down behind his workbench, essentially ending the conversion.

Shit. Shit. Shit. She pressed too far.

"Roy, please don't be angry with me." She couldn't handle him upset with her or the possibility of losing his friendship. Hannah had no one but Roy. He was the only person in her life concerned for her well being, her health, her happiness. If she lost him, she'd be alone. Screw the jewelry store and the plan if it meant that much to him.

"I can't lose you to some stupid idea that you're not thinking clearly," Roy said softly. "I can't lose you over a jewelry story that you have no business considering heisting. You're the only person in my life. I can't lose you. Period."

Hannah wrapped her arms around Roy from behind and leaned her cheek against his. Roy stuck by her through all of her insane shenanigans. His love, loyalty, and friendship couldn't be rivaled.

She caved. "I'll drop it."

He nodded but didn't reply.

She would drop the subject for Roy. His friendship trumped anything in her life. And he was right. Currently, there wasn't a good plan or scenario. But that didn't mean one wouldn't come to them eventually.

## 8

Jason handed his vacation request to Chief and waited. Chief didn't disappoint.

"You're asking for time off when we're knee-deep in a major case and I have to stave off the feds?"

"Yes."

Chief gave him a chastising stare, those nearly black eyes drilling holes into his skull. "Forget it."

His shoulders hunched. "I haven't taken a vacation in nearly three years. I'm burning out here, Chief."

Chief scrubbed a hand down his face. "Listen, I get it and I know I'm coming across as unreasonable. None of us have taken time off like we should." He sounded as zapped of all energy as Jason felt. "This case has us chasing our tails. What we have to assume is during the lull periods, she must be doing recon and strikes when she has her plan in place. It's her pattern. She hasn't given us a break. Let me see what I can do."

And for a moment, the chief almost sounded sympathetic. "But it would help if you solved this damn case."

Without a word, silence the best choice for the situation, as he might respond not so kindly, Jason turned and stalked out of Chief's office, slamming the door behind him. Purely out of frustration. Yeah, he should have predicted that response. Though he had hung a bit of hope that some time off in the near future would give him the rest he needed and deserved.

He went to his desk and tossed himself into his chair. A file sat front and center. Jason opened the folder to the still pictures of their jewelry thief along with stats—the worth of the items stolen, time stamps, locations of the stores, and any other detail they had, which wasn't much. They only managed to obtain a single twenty second video from outside one of the buildings after she'd done her deed. When they'd watched that surveillance video, her demeanor oozed calm and collected. A woman without fear of being caught. A dangerous trait.

She never appeared to be armed, but that didn't mean a weapon wasn't hidden somewhere on her person. Where, who knew? That skintight getup didn't leave much to the imagination. Even a blade would be noticeable. But they wouldn't know for sure until they could get a close up picture to analyze or finally arrest her.

He transfixed on a still shot from the last heist. A perfect silhouetted image, outlining an hourglass shape. If he didn't know better, he might have perceived the picture altered or fake. Frustrating, yet fascinating.

Yeah, Jason knew he'd gone too long without a woman in his life when he reduced himself to salivating over a picture. Ordinarily he left that gig to Dean. Seated at his work desk and drooling over a cat burglar didn't exude sensibility. Fucking hell.

Thinking hard about his social life, how long had it been since he had a date or took a woman to bed? Two years? He half-heartedly recalled his history timeline. Had it really been that long? His last girlfriend, an airline stewardess, stated vehemently she wanted a diamond ring and marriage. He'd been a jackass and strung her along for three years before she finally cut him loose. They'd had fun together during his courtship, but she just didn't do it for him to consider a forever tag. After that, he watched Nick get destroyed by a divorce. The man's wife was not able to handle being married to a cop. Less than five years of marriage and Nick's relationship didn't end civilly. Jason threw himself into his work after being a spectator to Nick's ordeal, avoiding the same type of relation hazard. A personal life didn't enter the picture. But now he realized what a mistake it'd been not to indulge. No wonder Dean never fretted. The man always took time to enjoy himself, no matter how many hours he worked. Some might suggest Dean lost himself in women nightly as he continued to internally grieve over his deceased wife.

Jason grumbled, closed the folder, and rubbed the back of his neck, suffering from bound up knots.

"Here." Dean set a large coffee in front of him. "You need this."

Yeah, he did.

"Turned you down, huh?"

"Yeah. Sort of. I don't know." He took a sip of the hot brew, allowing it to burn down his throat and slowly wake his tired body. Dean warned him Chief would refuse. But Jason ignored his partner. How could he get a vacation if he didn't ask?

"Listen, I know when you were first promoted you busted your ass to prove yourself. But you've also worked yourself into the ground. I warned you back then about doing that," his partner reminded him.

He'd never live down not taking the man's advice.

"Yeah, yeah."

"Don't brush me off, I'm not your girlfriend. I'm your partner. And when we're out there together and if things go bad for some reason, I have to be able to know that you're not too fucking tired to have my back. Now, go home on time today, and every other day, and take care of yourself." Dean's words turned gruff. A rare tone for the man. Which meant Jason hit a sore spot with his partner. The kicker? Dean wasn't wrong. He needed to be reliable if shit hit the fan. He never wanted to be responsible for any one of his LEO brothers or civilians getting hurt. An exhausted officer or detective could be a detriment to society.

"All right," he conceded.

"Go visit your parents and for God's sake, get laid." Dean strolled off, taking his cocky ass attitude with him.

With his partner's suggestion, Jason envisioned a saucy redhead. Briefly, he wondered how the hell he went about finding her. She captivated him enough to explore whether or not she could become a satisfying distraction.

## 9

Hannah strolled around the department store, a stack of jeans, T-shirts, and workout clothes piled in her arms. Her body changed rapidly, where a new wardrobe every couple months became an exciting shopping trip.

As she roamed around, lazily going through the racks, her mind wandered to McIntyre's, the sexy detective, and Roy. Too many ideas, thoughts, and plans laid out there with a plethora of possibilities. Good and bad. Fear of the men who her parents consistently borrowed money from always plagued her. Would she have enough cash to pay for the next debt if they found her? Scratch that, *when* they found her. Those men always, inevitably tracked her down. She did a quick mental calculation of her hidden cash.

Hannah stockpiled plenty of money for those guaranteed surprise visits. But that would be all, considering her parents never borrowed small. Idly, while she rummaged through a rack of clothing, she wondered if Carl could help her with those men who sought her for payment? She knew the man had significant mob connections.

The major issue with going to her buyer was she'd be asking him a favor and in return would owe him a favor. That's how these men worked. She fully understood the give and take. After all, her parents dealt with the same type of organized crime. Except Carl seemed to be on a higher tier of the mob. If that made sense. If she went to Carl with her issues, she'd insert herself directly into a world that she constantly fought to get away from.

She caught sight of a lovely red cocktail dress and contemplated the price tag. Perfect. For what, who knew? Hannah didn't go out anywhere or with anyone to make use of the lovely item. She added the dress onto her pile.

"Jason, I need to buy your father a new dress shirt and tie for your cousin's wedding in two weeks," a feminine voice said behind her.

"Mom, you're killing me," a semi-familiar voice countered.

Hannah glanced over her shoulder and did a double take. The cop who cornered her in the coffee shop tagged along behind an attractive older woman. His arms loaded down with bags, he looked like a grown son being tortured by his mother. Absolutely miserable. Hannah barked out a laugh, unable to help herself.

The cop's gaze swung her direction. A flash of surprise crossed his sharp facial features. Square jaw, a nose that clearly had been broken a time or two, unusually high cheekbones for a man, and ice blue eyes lined heavily with thick, dark lashes. Really, he was too beautiful.

A sly grin crossed over his face. He veered from the woman and made a beeline path straight for her.

"Having a good time?" she asked.

He looked entirely perturbed. "Don't all men love shopping with their mothers?"

"None that I know of."

"Yeah, I don't know of any, either."

Hannah went to make a jab at him but became captivated in the balletic woman descending upon them.

"Jason." His mother approached from behind. "I turned around and you weren't there. You had me worried."

"Mom, I'm a detective. I can protect myself." His mouth curled upward, simultaneously exasperated and amused.

"Yes, yes, I know." His mom stepped up next to him. "Are you going to introduce me to your friend?"

Jason rolled his eyes, opened his mouth, then clamped it shut. Probably realizing he didn't know her name. Ironically, he consumed Hannah's thoughts for the past couple weeks since the coffee shop meeting but she didn't know a single detail about him.

"Hannah." She held out her free hand. "Hannah Lakely." No, the name wasn't exactly stellar, but it was so odd, most people couldn't remember. They might recall Hannah, but the last name would always slip.

"Hello, Hannah. Beverly Campbell. It's nice to meet a female friend of Jason's." His mother was evidently clueless they didn't know each other.

"Friend?" She opted for some fun. "Your son arrested me for shoplifting last week. He was kind of an ass."

Jason gaped wordlessly.

His mother blinked, then grinned supremely. "You're a pistol. I like you. You should join us for lunch."

Hannah smirked when Jason turned to his mother, astonished. "Mom, you can't just go around inviting strangers to lunch. Especially when she said I arrested her."

"Did you arrest her?" his mother asked.

"No." He shot her a glare. "She thinks that's funny. She's seriously wrong."

His mother laughed, the pitch musical and light.

"I know, darling. Despite my wretched elderly age, I'm slightly lucid." His mother's obvious sarcasm was superb.

Jason huffed. "I never said—"

His mother shifted focus to her. "I have too much fun at my serious son's expense. He needs to lighten up."

"I couldn't agree more." Hannah winked playfully.

*　*　*

After Hannah escaped from her parents' home, she found herself in many odd situations to the point where she'd grown used to foreign sensations. But seated across from an unknown-to-her detective and his mother topped the list. She sat in awe of the unfiltered woman, who truly seemed to take pleasure in embarrassing her son but with a profound obvious affection. Each time Beverly looked at her son, the evident unconditional love radiated outward. And it pained Hannah. A few times she had to look away, afraid of the wanting expression that might cross her face. How different would her life have turned out if her mother remotely resembled Beverly Campbell? How would it feel to have the warmth and indisputable love of a parent?

Hannah forced herself to stomp on those emotions that threatened to expose a weakness she loathed. She was grown. Wishing and wanting for something that never existed in her life was futile.

"So Hannah, what do you do for a living?" Beverly asked.

A question she didn't often get asked, but one she was prepared for. "I'm a representative in merchandise distribution."

"What type of merchandise?" Jason plopped an onion ring into his mouth.

"Whatever I can get my hands on and I think will be easily moved. It's all about knowing the products. What can be sold on the street, so to speak. I'm actually very good at it. It takes a certain knack to understand the market and know what products won't sell or can't be unloaded. So instead of items sitting in my pocket, not able to be distributed, I make certain that each item I choose is wanted by buyers." Hannah answered truthfully, without adding that the items were stolen jewels. Only a tiny detail, right?

"How interesting. You must have to keep up on current trends," Beverly said.

"Exactly." Absently she moved her salad around her dish. "The great thing is that my job can be done from anywhere. I'm not stuck in an office Monday through Friday, nine to five."

Jason eyed her as she spoke. Specifically, he zeroed in on her eyes. That didn't deter him from filling his stomach with the restaurant's fried appetizers. It unnerved her how he expertly popped food into his mouth without breaking his steely gaze. She tramped down the sudden urge to squirm in her seat. Cops tended to pick up on those telling nuances.

"Did you have to go to school for that career?" Beverly asked.

She shook her head. "No, it's more about learning as you go and studying those around you. A lot of online research. I had some fantastic trainers."

She considered herself an expert at direct eye contact and giving them a truckload of bull. A skill she spent many hours practicing. One she used on quite a few people. She had to. It was truly difficult staring someone in the eye and boldface lying. Especially for someone like her who did have a conscience. It was a fine line to walk day in and day out. She learned to develop the skill by watching online videos and taking online psychology workshops that specifically dealt with lying. At the beginning, she had to keep herself in check from consistently fibbing to Roy. Now she'd grown, utilizing the skill on the appropriate individuals and times. Talk about a constant balancing act.

It was past time to change the subject away from her. Too many questions only led to more lies. "So how long have you been a cop?"

He cleared his throat. "Detective."

"He was promoted four years ago," Beverly bragged. "His father and I are extremely proud of him. But he's done nothing but work and runs himself ragged. Doesn't even take the time to come home and visit his parents."

"Mom," he scolded. "Not in front of strangers."

Hannah chuckled and toyed with her silverware.

"So you're a detective." Too tempting not to jab. She sent him a genial smile. "Aren't detectives usually...older?"

He coughed out the sip of Pepsi he took. "That's awfully presumptuous."

"Am I wrong?" She batted her lashes innocently.

He pursed his lips into a thin line. "No. But our group of detectives are all around my age."

"And that would be?"

"Thirty-four."

He appeared younger. She would have guessed twenty-eight or nine. At that moment, Roy's warning suddenly rang in her head. The realization she was playing a dangerous game washed over her. She shouldn't be seated at lunch with a detective and his mother. Time to walk away before she put herself into a horrible situation. Well, more so than she currently placed herself in. Nothing like a blond-haired, blue-eyed sexy man with a badge to scramble a woman's brain.

She made a show of glancing at her watch as an excuse. "I have to get going. I'm due to take a call in the next half an hour."

She grabbed her bags and scooted from the booth.

"Oh." She apparently shocked Beverly by her hasty and rude departure. "Thank you for joining us for lunch. Please let Jason walk you to your car."

"No, no. That's unnecessary. I can see myself out." She reached for her purse to pull out money.

Jason's large palm covered hers. The moment they connected, everything around her stopped. His warmth sent a succulent current over her. His light touch, she could imagine caressing her naked body, callused fingers creating a potentially delicious tingle in their wake. A sense of comfort swirled around her.

Hannah stood cemented in place, her gaze locked with his. His blue eyes dilated and his breath hitched at the same time hers did. He took a step closer, her chest brushing against the top of his stomach. His thumb lightly grazed the top of her hand in a slow circular motion. An exquisite scent of musk combined with Jason's natural masculinity wafted upward and wrapped around her. She wet her lips. His eyes darted to her lips and back up to her eyes. How would those lips feel tangling with hers? Or skimming up her bare spine? Or inside her thighs?

Jason's overpowering presence created a brain malfunction that had her mind going to a large bed, naked bodies, and a significant amount of kissing. Yeah. Kissing. She loved to kiss. Nothing like a good lip lock to make a woman melt.

How long they stood there, she didn't know. But she balked first. She jerked her hand away, breaking the spell. Hannah wholeheartedly accepted the ideology of instant attraction, but the last thing she needed was to indulge in a fling with a law enforcement officer who could potentially become her demise.

"I've got lunch." Jason's voice was hampered by a frog stuck in his throat.

"Thank you." She spun and rushed out of the restaurant.

When she reached her car and chucked the bags into the trunk, she took a deep cleansing breath to rid herself of the unwanted fog Jason created. She needed to keep a crystal clear mind. Involving herself in any relationship at this time didn't suggest a grand plan.

Hannah started her car and fled the mall parking lot, determined to forget about the sexy, handsome cop and his humorous mother.

## 10

Jason stood outside at the mall exit and watched Hannah climb into a Roadster. Talk about doing well for herself. A nice ride on the luxury side of vehicles.

She moved fluidly, an entrancing notable assuredness. Her flaming red hair flew behind her as she'd rushed from the building. Jason understood why. That slight touch between them sent all his rationale into a tailspin. The soft skin of her hand felt like silk beneath his rough fingers. Immediately, visions of running his palms over her naked form assaulted him. Inappropriate while seated next to his mother. Jason didn't understand the sensation, having never experienced it before. Thank goodness Hannah possessed the wherewithal to break the trance. The nitwit that he was, he'd have stayed frozen in that position for hours.

When she fled, more or less dismissing him and his mother, he tried to chase her down and ask for a phone number, a date, hell, another lunch. She hadn't given him an opportunity. She was damn fast for a tiny thing.

He shoved his hands into his pants pockets and watched her peel out of the parking lot, making note of her license plate and shaking his head at her erratic driving. He strolled back to the restaurant to find his mother paying for lunch.

"Mom," he protested.

"Oh, honey. It's all right for your mother to pick up the tab for lunch with her only son." Her blue eyes shined. He inherited those hues from his mother. Jason's family and friends always said he couldn't hide shit with his expressive eyes. Something he detested. Especially when he became a LEO, hiding his anger, surprise, and joy was a job necessity. Countless times Chief and his brothers nailed him for that trait deficiency. To this second he continued to work on that chink in his armor.

Jason grabbed his mother's shopping bags and they meandered through the mall to his car.

"Did you get her phone number?"

He suppressed a laugh. His mom, the unsuccessful matchmaker to her only son. "She hurried like her hair was on fire."

"Jason, how do you ever expect to settle down if you don't chase a good one?"

"Mom, why are you so set on marrying me off?" Sliding a ring onto a woman's finger did not make his bucket list.

His saint-of-a-mother smiled at him with nothing but love and affection. "A mother always wants to see her son happy and settled with a nice woman. I don't like you coming home to an empty house. And your father and I would like to have grandkids. Since you're my only son, I don't think that's unreasonable to ask, is it?"

"Well, yeah," he sputtered. Grandkids? For God's sake.

"Did you get her license plate number?"

His mother knew him too well. Despite what he said, Hannah captured his interest enough to pursue. "Yes."

"Good. You can track her down."

"Mom, she was nice, and all, but I don't know her. She could be some crazy woman with a rap sheet a mile long." His mother knew this, being married to a career cop. Sometimes her intrusion was mind-boggling. "Not only that, when she finds out that I ran her license plate and did a background check on her, that's not exactly a great way to start any type of relationship. Short term or long term. I'm not hunting a suspect but odds are she'll perceive it that way."

"You won't know unless you find her and ask." They approached his car and shoved the packages into the backseat. "I will agree with the background check. You do have to be careful who you date and in today's age, you need to take extra precautions."

"Mom." He closed the door, spun and placed his hands on her slim shoulders. "You know I love you. But you need to stop. When and if it happens, it happens. And you will most certainly be the first to know."

She smiled tenderly and patted his cheek. "Of course I will."

She slid in to the car and shut the door. Jason shook his head. If he didn't love his mother so damn much, she'd drive him crazy.

*** 

Jason held Hannah's information in his hands, unsure what exactly he wanted to do with it. Address, phone number, height, and weight. She'd clearly lost a significant amount of weight since that last DMV photo. He raked a hand over his buzz cut as he drifted back to his desk, coffee and muffin in his opposite hand.

Three days after bumping into Hannah and the sexy-as-sin woman riddled his thoughts. Her quick wit and sarcasm he admired. Her enormous sapphire blue eyes called to him like a siren. And her devilish grin had him wondering what shenanigans she devised in that gorgeous head.

"Campbell," Chief called from his office. "Get in here."

Jason moaned, veered off route from his desk and went straight to the boss's office.

"We got something off the last robbery. A hair. I've sent it to the lab. I asked them to rush the results which probably won't be back for a week or two." Chief plunked down in the chair behind his large metal desk, picked up his coffee mug and took a long swig.

"Where did you get that?" He pointed to Jason's pastry.

"Break room."

Chief picked up his phone and barked at Tyler to put his name on a muffin before they all disappeared.

"What's the hair color?"

"Blonde." Chief slammed the receiver back down.

Jason exhaled, frustrated. That didn't give them much and, until the lab got the results back, the small amount of information didn't get them any closer to their burglar. DNA might help if a match already existed in the system.

"I feel ya," Chief said.

"Where did they find the hair?"

"On a piece of broken glass."

"Any blood?" That would be a golden piece of evidence. That blonde hair could have come from anyone working or visiting the store and might be a coincidence. But blood on broken glass could only link one person, their perp.

Chief's taut face told him the news wouldn't be the answer he sought. "Sorry, buddy. We're going to have to keep working at this until we catch a break."

"She's smart. She's no fool and she has to have help on the outside. We're missing something. We have to be. No criminal is this perfect." He shoved Hannah's papers into his jacket pocket.

"I agree, but so far she's done well to cover her tracks. Mistakes will be made. We just have to be sure we're there to pick up on her blunders and before something goes wrong." Chief opened up a folder. "McIntyre's refusal to cooperate doesn't help."

"She'd be stupid to go after that place." Part of Jason hoped their jewelry thief wasn't planning to hit the infamous store. Nothing like trigger happy rent-a-cops to start raining gunfire as soon as they caught sight of her. There'd be nothing Jason or the team could do for her. Jason concluded the reason McIntyre's didn't want to cooperate was they hoped to nab the stealthy thief themselves. The headlines that could garner for the jeweler would increase business significantly. A great PR stunt. A nightmare for the detectives working the case.

"Not stupid, greedy. There's a difference. And who knows why she's greedy. She's had to have grossed plenty of money off the stolen gems. We haven't tracked down one item on the street. She knows exactly what she's going after. No engraved or specially marked pieces. Only loose diamonds and rubies worth a pretty penny, along with some loose strand pearls. Greed inflates a person's ego and will lead to errors. She may be good, but you're right, she's not perfect. Greed will be her downfall one way or another. We just need to hope no blood is shed in the process. So far, no one has been injured and we're lucky that's the case." Chief slammed the folder shut. "I have a bad feeling about this one. We need to catch her before it all goes to hell, including the feds walking through the front door."

Chief wasn't telling him something he didn't already know. Except how does one go about finding a needle in a haystack when said needle disguises herself as a piece of the haystack? Clearly, their perp was blending in well with the world around her.

## 11

Hannah's body turned to jelly. Her arms ached from lifting a significant amount of weight to build her strength. Her thighs trembled from benching twice her body weight. Her stomach ached from so many crunches she lost count. Her feet tingled from the crushing punishment she put on them by pounding on a treadmill. She'd be genuinely surprised if she could walk out of the gym.

"Push it, Lakely." Her brutal trainer positioned himself beside the treadmill and barked words of what he considered encouragement. The asshole.

The man was a well respected, retired local boxer. When she first scheduled to meet him, she figured the title retired meant sixties. Nope, forty and good looking as sin. Still, she wanted to kick his ass for the torture he put her through. Her body wanted to crumble from soreness and weakness.

Wherever Hannah established residence, she found a gym and sought out a personal coach to kick her butt. If she didn't, she wouldn't be in the shape she needed to pull off her robberies. Or defend herself. Some trainers had been great. Some, not so much. This one she titled the *Bane of Her Existence*.

"Five more minutes since you've decided to be a pansy-ass today." He reached up and added the time. She smacked his hand. He added two more minutes. Fucking bastard.

She finished what she perceived to be an extra forty-five minutes, not seven, and her trainer handed her a bottle of water and a protein shake. He patted her on the back and went off to his next victim. It took her a half an hour to gingerly limp out of the gym.

After her workout session, she intended to do a bit of scouting on a new jewelry store a town over. A neat little plan Roy cooked up to throw the police for a loop. A small shop, located right on Route 30, created an easy getaway. Really, the job was small fries compared to her current capabilities. But Roy brought to her attention a good assessment, the small heist might send the cops into a state of confusion, trying to pin a pattern. But Hannah's body was destroyed. A hard body slam to the mat that knocked the wind out of her during her self-defense training and it'd been difficult to fully recuperate. Her trainer yelled at her the entire time to suck it up. Which she honestly tried. Now she just wanted to soak in her spa tub and melt the aches and pains away.

Hannah pulled her car into her assigned spot of the apartment building, grabbed her gym bag, and plodded her way up to the seventh floor. When she stepped out of the elevator, she stopped, the bag slipped from her shoulder.

Fuck.

Jason's head popped up her direction from the phone he had been browsing. He pushed off the wall he'd been leaning against just outside her apartment door.

Had the police figured her out?

She took a retreated step, ready to bolt.

But Jason smiled and lifted his hand, taking her aback. "I've been waiting for you."

Why?

"How did you find me?" Another sly step toward the stairwell located to the left of the elevator. Her eyes darted the hallway and surrounding closed doors to the other apartments, anticipating police backup.

He shoved his phone into his pocket and approached her. Dressed in what she assumed was a police regulation suit, he wore it too well. The dark blue color enhanced his eyes. Add the military haircut, larger than life physique, and broad shoulders, he exuded both intimidating and sexy. "DMV," he said. "Address and phone. I considered calling first but not recognizing my number, I was afraid you might not answer."

Her eyes scanned the hallway again. Where were the rest of the police hiding? It was possible someone might be positioned in the stairs. Crap. Cornered. The walls closed in on her. Her blood rapidly pulsed as she allowed panic to creep in. She glanced at the window located at the end of the hall. No. Sixth floor equaled severe injuries.

"I know I'm not supposed to use my connections for such things, but you skipped out on lunch the other day before I had the chance to ask for your number." He gave her an easygoing smile.

What? Her bag hit the floor with a thud.

Jason bent over, picked it up, and held it out for her.

"I don't understand." Her mind raced with a million thoughts at once. Something didn't fit. Something was off. He couldn't be asking her out. He came to arrest her. Right?

He tilted his head, puzzled. "I wondered if you'd like to go to dinner. A couple drinks, a movie. You know, the whole date thing." He stopped and an awkward embarrassment creased his brow. "You are single, right? Geez, I hope I didn't misread you."

She burst out laughing, relief coursing through her. Her body sagged. Blood pumped in her ears and her heart beat erratically. Jason had no intention on busting her. He was floundering, asking her out on a date. The realization came across endearing and disturbing.

"Yes, I'm single." But she couldn't go out with him. "I'm sorry, Jason, I'm just not dating right now."

His brows slid together. "Why? Bad breakup?"

Why did it always have to be about another man? It couldn't be that she enjoyed being single? That she didn't mind the wretched loneliness? That she enjoyed eating out at restaurants by herself? That she loved getting hit on at a bar every time she sat down to enjoy a beer?

"No." She honed her female fortitude and squared her shoulders. "I'm afraid I don't have the time to invest in any form of relationship."

His eyes grew huge. Hannah thought she heard a choking type noise come from him. "Good lord, I'm not asking for a relationship. I'm asking for dinner."

The air went out of her spunk. She pointed to him. "I think I saw your eye tic."

"Did it? A natural reaction when I get the crap scared out of me by a woman," he said, slapping a hand over his right eye. "Dinner. Drinks. Movie." He ticked off on his hand. "This doesn't have to be some grand life moment. A night out to enjoy."

Tempting. It had been a few years since she went on a date or enjoyed company while at the movies.

And he was right, it didn't have to be some great life epiphany that changed her forever. She could have dinner with the officer, no strings attached. They would part ways as acquaintances with the occasional phone conversation here or there to stay in touch. No more, no less. She wouldn't compromise herself or Roy.

Jason awaited expectantly, his eyes giving away a bit of vulnerability that she might actually turn him down. She should.

"All right." She caved. She blamed his blue eyes.

His features lit up with a wide grin that transformed him, looking much younger and relaxed. Why didn't he have women swooning at his feet? Why wasn't he already scooped up by some blonde bombshell of a housewife?

"Terrific." Jason handed her the tote. "I'll pick you up Saturday at seven."

"Okay."

Jason reached past her and punched the call button on the elevator. "I look forward to it."

Before he asked for another unreasonable request, she scurried to her apartment and let herself inside. Fucking hell. She accepted a date with a cop.

## 12

"It's a wig?" Jason asked. "She's wearing a wig?"

Chief grumbled something incoherent. He held up the report with the findings. "Obviously she's wearing a wig as part of her disguise. She's smart enough to try and protect her natural hair from getting loose under her full head mask. Damn it, she's savvy."

Dean smirked. "All the more reason to admire the beauty."

Tyler huffed. "She's not beautiful. She's a criminal. One who needs brought to justice."

"Whoa, boy. Settle down the by-the-book propaganda machine." Dean baited the overzealous detective. Technically his age difference only spanned five years. Tyler's younger age was a result of not going through the normal bullshit years the rest of the team had to in order to make detective.

Tyler, the classic rookie detective of the group, constantly tried to prove himself worthy of the title. Too gung-ho on catching their perp. It was an unspoken, well-known fact that Tyler obtained detective status from political connections. He came from a family of career-bred politicians—his father, a state senator, rumored to be considering a run for governor of Pennsylvania; his mother, the quintessential politician's wife; his sister, an advisor for their father.

Essentially a good kid, Tyler's all-business-all-the-time persona tended to get in his own way. But they all kept him reined in. If they didn't, he could possibly make a mistake and end up compromising a case or hurting someone or himself.

"We *will* catch her." Chief stared poignantly at Tyler. "But we'll do it smart and without incident."

Obviously feeling chastised, Tyler slumped back in his chair, his face red.

"How did you get the results so fast?" Jason asked.

Dean read over the report, a mischievous spark in his eye. "The cutie in lab has a thing for Chief."

Their boss rolled his eyes but noticeably didn't respond.

"We're once again with nothing." Jason bounced the pen off the yellow leg pad in front of him. How fucking frustrating.

"We'll get something," Dean said, with an underlying resolve. "They always screw up. Always."

\*\*\*

Jason walked into his parents' home, arms loaded with groceries and a six pack of beer for him and his father to split. When he went to the mall with his mother the other day, she had managed to guilt-trip him that he didn't visit enough, which he couldn't deny. He needed this afternoon to decompress. His parents normally helped when a case got under his skin.

"Did you get ketchup?" his father asked, plucking a beer out of Jason's hands.

"Yeah. How did you run out of ketchup? Isn't it a staple of your diet?" Jason mocked.

"Said the child who ate ketchup sandwiches." His dad rummaged through the utensil drawer and found a metal spatula.

Jason set the bag on the counter and pulled out the condiment bottle. His dad snatched it out of his hands and hurried outside to the grill. His mom entered the kitchen and he leaned down to kiss her cheek.

"That man has been itching for you to get here so he could play with his new grill. Boys and their toys." His mom smiled cheerfully.

"Why are you grilling out for just the three of us?"

"Oh no, the neighbors are coming over in a bit. There'll be about ten of us here. The Waid's daughter is home from school, she'll be here, as well. And she's single." Mention of the neighbor's daughter by his mother was not meant to be casual.

He internally groaned. The woman would not give up. "Mom, I do not need you setting me up."

"I'd like to have a daughter-in-law."

"As you've said every time you see me. Seriously, it's over the top." Jason twisted the cap off a longneck. "Not every woman is cut out to be a detective's wife. It takes a special personality and temperament to marry one of us. You, of all people, should know."

His mom tsked as she pulled out containers of pasta and macaroni salad. "I realize that. The last thing I want for you is to be in a marriage where your wife can't handle your job."

"Why does it have to be marriage? Why go straight to the altar? Good lord, Mother." A second woman in the matter of twenty four hours mentioning commitment and/or marriage had him developing a weird eye spasm. Soon he'd need to seek medical attention for the twitch. "And I do have a date on Saturday." There, throw her a bone.

"You do? With whom?" He swore he saw little wedding doves fly in circles above his mother's head.

"Hannah. I got her info and tracked her down. I'm taking her to dinner and a movie." He snatched a fork out of the silverware drawer and scooped out a pile of pasta. He moaned as the savory salad hit his tongue. Home cooking beat store made in any contest. He needed to make a point to visit his parents more often.

His mom spooned a heap of the macaroni salad into a bowl. Jason snagged the food and shoveled it in, starving.

"You be a gentleman, Jason. Treat her with respect." She wielded a pink painted fingernail at him.

He saluted. "Yes, ma'am. And I'm ending this conversation now."

Jason went outside to watch his father play with his shiny, new grill.

"What's going on, son?" Straight to the point, always.

Yeah, his father saw right through him. Years on the force trained his dad to be an extremely observant man. Rarely, did anything get by the man.

Jason shrugged and took a swig of his beer.

"How's Dean?"

"He's doing okay." Really, his partner was anything but fine, but Jason refused to judge or interfere unless Dean became a threat to himself or his brothers.

His father chuffed. "That's a blatant lie."

"He's doing as well as can be expected."

His dad nodded while placing burgers in a symmetrical line on the grill. "I don't know a man that could go through what he did and still walk around lucid. How's the jewelry thief case?"

There it was. His opening, gifted by his father who knew he wouldn't discuss the docket unless asked, to get some things off his chest. "It's going nowhere. We found a hair but turns out it was a wig strand. We have nothing and Chief is stressed that the feds will be walking in the door any minute."

"They will."

Damn his dad's matter of factness.

"Chief wants to prevent that from happening."

His father brushed the burgers with the ketchup. "Understandable, but probably unavoidable at this point. This case has been going on for a couple years. I'm sure the value of diamonds stolen is extensive. I'm just surprised they've taken this long."

Technically, Jason couldn't talk about the case, but his father could make educated guesses that were spot on.

His father flipped the burgers to brush the underside. "You'll catch her."

With those three words, a burden lifted off Jason's shoulders. He needed this. His father's confidence in him meant the world. Even though Chief said the same thing, his dad, a well respected former officer and retired member of their community, was never wrong.

## 13

Hannah gave herself a once over in the mirror. It'd been a long time since she dressed up for a date. She kept a low key profile in all aspects of her life. A necessity to avoid questions from those she came into contact with.

She finger combed her hair and straightened her white form fitted tee. She wore a long, flowing black skirt and a pair of flats. Always flats. She swooned over heels, but they weren't conducive to abrupt escapes.

At precisely seven, a firm rap on her apartment door alerted her to Jason's arrival. Naturally, he was punctual.

Hannah glanced through the peep hole. Hell.

She rested her forehead against the door and closed her eyes. Trouble stood on the other side. Big. Time. Trouble.

Another knock.

Taking a deep breath, she swung open the door. Dark washed blue jeans, a black T-shirt that clung to his developed body, a black pair of slip on casual shoes, and a black Columbia jacket, Jason was dressed as every woman's delicious dream man. When he grinned, his features lightened dramatically, showing off a hint of boyishness.

"Hi," he said.

"Hi."

"You ready?"

"Let me grab my jacket and purse." Hannah moved aside and welcomed him into her apartment. If she didn't want to raise suspicion, she needed to be polite. It wasn't as if she invited him for dinner or to stay the night, where he might find some questionable objects located in her bedroom. Like a floor plan to a jewelry store she'd been studying. A step into the living room area wouldn't compromise her.

She hurried back to her spacious bedroom and grabbed her items. When she returned to the living room, Jason stood at the bay window, staring out over the evening city skyline.

"How on earth did you get this apartment?"

She sometimes forgot how lucky she had it, living in the upscale apartment. "Completely by accident."

She stepped up next to him, admiring the sun setting behind the tall buildings, the yellows and oranges bouncing off the mirrored windows of the skyscrapers. "I happened to be viewing an apartment two buildings down when I bumped into the building manager. I sweet talked him into giving me first dibs on the place."

He chuckled and shoved his hands into his jeans pockets. "I can imagine."

He slid her a side glance, his height towering her. She loved tall men. They made her feel safe and cherished when they wrapped a protective arm around her small frame. That sentiment never lasted, as she couldn't allow herself to become attached.

"You have everything?" he asked.

"Yep."

"Great, let's get this done and over with."

Her mouth dropped open, astonished. Why the hell would he ask her out if it was going to be a chore?

His mouth curved upward and he laughed—a deep manly rumble, bubbling from his chest. "Kidding. Let's go so I can wine and dine you, m' lady."

Jerk.

Jason held out his arm and she looped her hand through his, but not before gifting him a swift punch to his gut. Nothing too harmful. He bent over slightly at the contact. "I deserved that."

"Yes, you did."

\*\*\*

Hannah couldn't remember when she enjoyed a date, without a care in the world. Instead of starting off the evening with dinner, Jason insisted they begin with the movie. A comedy. Since she hadn't eaten, she claimed she needed a large tub of popcorn to snack on. Payback for his earlier snip. She enjoyed the snack until her stomach became upset from the saturated butter. So much for revenge. Luckily, she carried antacid in her purse. After the movie, they sat at the bar of a far-from-intimate chain restaurant for a couple drinks before they were seated for their meals. The setting worked for her. Rapid background activity and noise took away the possibility of a romantic ambiance.

"Why did you decide to become a police officer?" she asked.

"My family has a long history of military and police. Naturally, it's the first profession I chose for a potential career." He cut into his thick steak.

"Do you have any sisters or brothers?"

"No, I'm an only child to a meddlesome mother and an overactive father." His eyes lit with amusement. "I do have many cousins. My mother has two sisters and a brother and my father has three brothers."

"Wow, such a large family." A twinge of sadness encompassed her. She never had the benefits of a sibling to have someone to hold onto for survival. She would never have a large family unit. Reunions, barbeques, weddings, anniversaries, birthdays hadn't, and never would, exist in her world. Only grungy neighbors yelling across the courtyard to one another to turn down the televisions or the kids living in the apartments beating the hell out of each other. And the occasional loan shark knocking on her parents' door. Real family bonding moments.

"Yeah. Do you have any sisters or brothers?" He took a bite of his steak.

Hannah pushed around her chicken fettuccini alfredo, her appetite diminishing. "No, I'm an only child, as well."

"Sorry." He astutely picked up on her melancholy.

"Don't be. It's not something I can control, right?" She forced a smile.

"Where are your parents?" he asked. "Are you from around here?"

She shook her head. Here came the tricky part. Only two people knew anything about her. Roy and Carl, who did a very thorough, unwelcomed background check on her. She never confessed her history to anyone. Not that she got close enough to people to have that intimate detailed conversation.

But every once in a while, a topic came up in random casual discussions with acquaintances. She learned telling a version of the truth kept her from having to remember fibs and stories.

"I'm not from around here," she said. "Originally, I lived in upstate New York, but moved here to get away from my parents."

Jason lowered his fork, his small smile turned downward. "Why?"

"Drug addicts. They're constantly in trouble with loan sharks, borrowing money for their next fix. The last straw was when three large men came to the house to collect. It wasn't my parents' legs that got broken." All true. She remembered the day vividly. Often she woke in middle of the night, screaming from the memory of the pain as the baseball bat connected with her shin. She hadn't been strong enough to fight off the two men who held her.

"Hannah." Jason's voice filled with sympathy.

Her head snapped up. "Don't," she bit out harshly. "Don't pity me, Jason. I've left that life and won't allow my parents to affect me any longer. I've taken control. I realized at that moment, if they could watch their only daughter pay for their indiscretions and not change their ways, they were lost parents, people, humans. However you wish to classify them. After I got out of the hospital, I picked up the few items I had and left and I'll never look back. It was the best and easiest decision I ever made."

He set down his fork and folded his hands above his plate. They remained silent for a long time. She glaring at him. Him studying her.

Finally he spoke, his tone soft and soothing. "A lot of people in your position end up victims of their parents' poor choices. They fall into a repeat pattern, where continuing the vicious cycle is what's norm for them. You've managed to get yourself free and clear. That's commendable, Hannah, and shows an inner strength you should be proud of."

She went to reply with sarcasm but had nothing. Hannah clamped her mouth and glanced away, squashing the slight, undesirable feeling of relief of his acceptance. When it came down to it, it didn't matter if Jason saw her as a survivor. It didn't matter who thought what of her. She did what it took to pull herself out of her parents' grip. A path bound to get her either maimed or killed. She refused to regret her decisions or bask in other's admiration of her survival.

She plastered on a smile. "So, your mother is quite a character."

He didn't take the bait, instead, stared her down. Those ice blue eyes burrowing into her.

Damn it. Right in front of her sat the issue of becoming involved with a cop. Their automatic nature refused to drop a topic or subject until they were satisfied with the outcome. They didn't easily veer off the trail, especially when they smelled blood in the water.

After a long, painful silent moment, he must have selected not to push her. "Yes, my mom is quite a woman. I couldn't have asked for a better mother. Oh, she nags, but she's also the first one to come to my defense and has supported me throughout every stupid mistake and every triumph."

Hannah could hear the pride seep through his tone. Having spent a brief amount of time with his mother, she understood why he exhibited such delight when speaking about her.

"And your father?"

Jason snorted. "My father's enjoying retirement. He'd been a LEO for thirty-five years. He's actually become obsessed with his barbeque grill."

"LEO?"

"Law enforcement officer."

"I didn't realize you guys gave yourselves nick names," she teased.

"Cute."

Hannah pushed her pasta around, finding her appetite entirely vanished. Despite how much she breezily conversed with Jason, she couldn't see him past tonight. Roy undoubtedly would throttle her, even after assuring him there'd be no repeat evening. For good reason. She regretted saying yes to Jason. He seemed like a decent guy and she only had one of those in her life. How much she would love to be surrounded by positive people in her life. Who knew for sure with one date if Jason truly was a wonderful man? He could be a serial killer posing as a cop. They tended to love their mothers, right?

"So your dad likes to grill," she said absently, focused on the thick sauce at the bottom of the pasta bowl.

Jason tapped his knife at the edge of her plate. "Hey, where'd you go?"

"Sorry."

He blew out a defeated breath and set down his utensils, again. "This isn't going well, is it?"

It would be so easy to answer with a lie. Tell him the entire date turned into a fiasco and they could end the night here and now. It would be best for both of them. But being completely honest with herself, so far she enjoyed their evening together, despite the heavy topic of her parents. Which she needed to shake off. She couldn't allow them to drag her down, even in horrific memories. Why did she always end up going back when she worked so damn hard to move forward?

Hannah closed her eyes briefly, pushed out all the crap, and chose to enjoy the remainder of their date.

"I'm having a good time, Jason," she said. "I'm sorry if you're not."

She purposely turned it around on him.

"No, no." His panicked expression was utterly ridiculous and priceless. "I've been having a great time."

She grinned, pleased with herself.

He narrowed his eyes when he realized what she'd done. "Funny. You're a funny, funny woman."

She burst out laughing, enjoying that Jason could handle her.

He picked up his fork and pegged her. "You are trouble."

"Who? Me?"

They finished dinner slowly, Hannah learning much more about Jason than he did her. He never asked her about her work, but she'd already given him that bit of false information. He didn't ask about friends after the topic of her parents came up. They did find out they had quite a bit in common, like their love to vacation at the beach. They both enjoyed working out at the gym and they both preferred to spend time at a home with a gathering of friends rather than going out to clubs or bars. Not that Hannah experienced that form of friendship festivity. She'd been forced to embrace becoming a loner due to her career choice.

Around eleven, Jason walked her to her apartment door and escorted her inside.

"Thank you for the lovely evening, Jason. I had a really nice time." She actually meant it. The date was relaxing, she had fun and enjoyed the company of a genuinely nice man. She even forgot his line of work at some point after dinner. He made it too easy to do.

Jason stood right inside the doorway and leaned against the wall. "I did, too."

What were his expectations? In a way, she hoped he didn't ask for a second date. But in another, she wanted him to. She didn't want to deny him. He gave her no excuse. Except his job in law enforcement conflicted with her lifestyle. Damn it.

"Can I kiss you goodnight?" He shifted his stance.

Speechless, she couldn't believe her ears. He asked? What the hell type of man was Jason? He asked to kiss her? That just didn't happen. Ever. Talk about old school.

She nodded, unable to form a non-quip answer to his question.

Jason pushed off the wall and took her around the waist. Slowly, he leaned down, his eyes bouncing from hers to her lips. She became mesmerized in his blues, noticing the black outline around the irises.

When his lips touched hers, he stole her breath. His hand snaked up her back to the nape of her neck and Hannah lost all sense of inhibition. She took the lead, her tongue sneaking out and swiping at his lips. Jason didn't hesitate. He devoured her, their kiss turning from a gentle goodbye to a passionate expression of need.

She let herself go and caved when he overtook the lead. She wilted under the carnal abandonment of releasing her guard enough to trust Jason and enjoy his control of their mutual hunger. She savored being a normal woman desired by a man who she found more than just a little attractive. She floated, all her angst gone under Jason's overwhelming power.

Jason pinned her against the wall. Her hands went to his shirt and yanked it out of his jeans. She needed to touch him. Feel him.

His temperature ran hot beneath her fingertips, his skin surprisingly silky as she glided her fingers over his lower back. Jason lifted her to wrap her legs around his waist. Their bodies grinded together, his erection punching through his jeans and hitting her in just the right spot. She broke free of his mouth and her head fell back against the wall, relishing the sensation. An unrecognizable moan escaped her throat. God, she wanted him inside her. She wanted to enjoy his naked body covering hers. Too long she'd gone without a man's sexual crave. She wanted his warmth to embrace her and thaw her. She was so cold. To her marrow. Jason's large body could make her feel human for once. One night of pure pleasure, the heat of a man beside her in bed, the sensation of his lips on her bare skin, the tangling of limbs, the sensuality emanating from both of them, giving in to their primal wants, to give her the excitement of being desired.

It was entirely selfish. And it would be a mistake. An enormous one. She couldn't afford to get intimately close to him. She couldn't take the chance he'd want to develop a relationship. Any form of intimacy was too close for comfort. Especially from Jason, a man tied to the law. Bound by an oath to serve and protect.

Hannah nudged Jason's chest. He immediately backed off, setting her down to stand on shaky feet and taking a step back. He raked a hand over his cropped hair, his chest unmistakably rising and falling to gain air. The loss of his heat gave room for the chill in the air to whip around her.

"I'm sorry." He cleared the catch in his throat, his apology gruff.

"Don't be." She straightened her shirt. "I can't say I didn't like it."

"Will you go out with me again?"

She was ready to deny him.

"Don't answer me now." He held up his hand and edged toward the door. "You want to say no, even after we had a great time tonight and you can sense this damn chemistry between us. Really think about it before you turn me down."

His expression implored. He leaned down, kissed her on the forehead, turned and stalked out of her apartment.

For fuck's sake. Trouble didn't cover the dilemma that now chased Hannah.

14

Jason picked up his cell to dial Hannah but set it back down, afraid of her response. For two days he debated calling her and for two days he consistently chickened out, like a fucking pansy. Pick up the phone, pull up her contact info, and change his mind—it was a torturous pattern.

He kneaded the palms of his hands into his eyes. What the hell did he do? Jason couldn't get her off his mind. This apprehension totally baffled him. After their date, he went home and tossed and turned all night. If Hannah hadn't pushed him away when she did, Jason would have hauled her to her bedroom and made love to her. Hannah was the real deal. Their date had become an unexpectedly refreshing event he never thought he'd experience with a woman. Truth be told, a woman he hadn't concerned himself with finding.

Hannah's confidence, quick wit, and sharp tongue proved she could hold her own with him. She wasn't a LEO bunny, hanging off the uniform. She didn't look to nab herself a cop. She went out to have a date and a good time and managed to take him along for the ride. Hannah made eye contact, a trait he insisted those around him possess. The only time she wavered was when she spoke about her parents. He understood. Those two dirt bags didn't deserve a daughter like Hannah—balanced, resilient, and independent. Her shame and embarrassment had seeped out when she reminisced over what she'd gone through. Jason was positive she hadn't touched on even a small part of what she'd experienced. That deep-seated instinct to protect her crept up. His need to haul her back to his home and place her in his care so no one could hurt her wanted to show its muscle. But he had an inkling going all crazy-protective on Hannah wouldn't fly. She'd probably bail. Her sour reaction to his empathy and her little speech that she prided herself on being strong and iron-willed and surviving gave enough of a warning. But it wouldn't kill her to lean on someone, would it? Hell if he knew.

Did he want to be that man? Yes, Jason wanted a second date. Yes, he wished to see and sit down to a pleasurable meal with her again. Warning flags rose as the realism of coveting another opportunity to spend time with Hannah struck a cord. A shudder slithered down his spine at the thought of a substantial relationship. He couldn't handle one. Had no inclination to jump into one. Not with his work schedule. He married his job. A relationship with a woman and she'd become the mistress.

"Hey." Dean strolled up and sat down on the corner of his desk. Why couldn't his partner sit his ass down in his own chair, located behind the desk right across from him? They got to look at each other for hours on end, *if* Dean decided to actually work.

"What's up?"

"I'm having a get together Saturday for the team and anyone else who'd like to join us. We're all beat to hell and it's time we relax. I got the go ahead from Chief. I think he's going to actually show."

A brilliant plan someone should have thought of months sooner. It'd been forever since any of them had unwinding downtime. Even a throwaway day to just kick back, have a few beers, and relax. He could bring Hannah.

"Can I bring someone?"

Dean rolled his eyes. "You can't bring your mom, man. We are drinking. Drink. Ing. No moms allowed."

Jason punched his partner in the arm. "Fuck you. My mom is awesome. But I'm talking about a date."

"A date?" Dean perked up. "Do tell."

What the hell did he say? "It's nothing really. I mean, I don't know if she'll even accept. We went out the other night and had a great time, but she's hesitant."

Dean's eyes narrowed. "Why? Because you're a cop? That's shitty. You run from her. We watched Nick go through hell and back over a woman who couldn't deal with his career."

"No." Jesus, why did he always think women centered around the badge? Okay, presumably with Dean, they did. "I'm not sure, but I think she's had a rough life and she has a wall, or something."

Dean clapped his hands together. "Walk away, man. Walk away. Women with baggage are too much trouble."

Annoyance riled him. How presumptuous and hypocritical of his partner. "The only baggage you come across is when you find out they're married."

His partner lifted his hands in a negligent manner. "Not my problem they can't get what they want at home."

"You're an asshole."

Dean stood and snatched his coffee cup. "I'm telling you, stay away from a woman with issues. It's never good, Jason."

His partner sauntered away, but not before flinging an arm over the emergency operator who just punched in to come on duty, and whispering into her ear.

Dean's advice on this one was reasonable. Should he walk away? Hannah gave him the obvious hint she would refuse a second date. But if he was honest with himself, their chemistry in that kiss, in the way she touched him, and in the way they melded together, wouldn't allow him to let go that easily. Nope. He'd contact her to see if she'd be willing to go to Dean's party. And if not, he'd have to reluctantly take Dean's warning. Perhaps. Depended on the conversation. Probably not. Damn it to hell.

## 15

"You went out with the cop!" Roy paced his living room, around his workbench, like a caged, irritated kitty. "And you didn't just go out with him, you kissed him. And you didn't just kiss him. You almost had sex with him."

Goddamn it. She constantly forgot about those stupid cameras Roy insisted she place in her apartment. She must have hit the remote on her key chain to activate the devices. A portable alert Roy cooked up. The equipment normally remained dormant and only switched on if she pressed the button on the mechanism. She hadn't used the accessory to-date, until yesterday.

When they'd deliberated the cameras for security reasons, she'd been extremely hesitant to allow anyone that private access. After a compelling argument on his part, citing her thievery and the mob, Roy managed to convince her that he could contact the police or Carl, in an extraordinary circumstance. With the power placed solely in her hands. Literally.

She held up her hand. "First, if you think that's coming close to having sex, we need to have a review about the birds and the bees–"

"You know what I mean!" Roy pulled on his hair, frustrated.

"I must have hit the remote by mistake. You weren't meant to see that kiss. Hell, I don't know what happened between Jason and me." She stood in his living room, her hands on her hips.

"I should have turned off the cameras immediately. I apologize. I did after a few minutes, when I knew you weren't being attacked and realized you must have accidentally hit the switch. But something's not right. I can't pinpoint my concern. I've been worried about you for the past few weeks. It doesn't help you've been focused on hitting McIntyre's." His head dropped on his shoulders.

Oh, hell. She didn't want Roy to question his uncanny instincts. Her friend possessed the ability to understand and acknowledge when something raised his hackles—a sixth sense warning of a threat of an unknown event on the horizon. She could not afford to have him hesitate for even a brief moment all because she ripped him a new one over her own stupid error.

Before her first heist in the area, Roy did the original research and kept her from approaching a possible buyer, someone named Sampson, to sell her stolen diamonds to. Turned out the notorious street thug would have likely double-crossed her and she'd end up a piece of floating debris in the Monongahela River. A few months ago, Sampson had been found dead in an apartment building in the city. The news had his gruesome death splattered as their headline story for two days. Roy found Carl with thorough online research of city news reports about the local syndicate and hacking of court records and documents. Roy even went as far as to tap into the files of the well known defense attorney that represented the entire clan of criminals. Roy gave his approval, accompanied with a strict warning to approach carefully. She never suspected Carl was willing to put a bullet into her head when she turned her back to leave his office. She had Roy to thank for leading her in the right direction.

"Hey." She lifted his head so he'd meet her eyes. "You don't need to apologize. This was my fault. You followed through by checking the video feed when it flipped on."

Oddly enough, the knowledge that someone watched her back comforted her. Utilizing technology, she wasn't alone. Despite that he remained a prisoner in his apartment, he managed to protect her like a sibling. And in return, she made certain Roy never retreated into loneliness.

He nodded.

She leaned up on her tip toes and kissed his cheek. "I need you to have my back. No one else does."

Roy relaxed with obvious relief.

"Jason cornered me." She went to the small, yellow kitchen and pulled out two bottles of water from the fridge. She handed one to Roy, along with his anti-anxiety medication.

"How?"

"I came home from the gym and he was waiting outside my apartment. I thought I was getting busted. Funny I forgot to hit the remote then. Which reminds me, I need to come up with an escape route if I ever get the police pounding on my door. I should probably move to a ground floor apartment."

"You just *had* to have a view," Roy groused. "At least the first floor has more exits."

Hannah shrugged, went back to the kitchen and took stock of his food supply. She explained the entire conversation between her and Jason, and summarized the date night. "He's really a good guy, that's what sucks. You know, he graduated at the top of his police academy class. He earned detective without political pull or having to know someone. Though odds are his dad being a retired officer had a bit to do with it. He owns a three bedroom home and his mother is adorable. He is the total package."

She flopped onto on the sofa.

"You like him," Roy accused.

"No." Hannah considered her response. "I'm in awe that such a man exists."

Roy slumped into his work station chair. "What does that mean?"

She didn't reply for a long time, processing an answer to best express what she did mean. "He seems like a man a woman could settle down with, take comfort in, depend on. Marry."

"As opposed to the egotistical womanizer or wife beater?" He stepped over the line by referencing her father.

"Yeah." She absorbed herself in the television screen, not having the energy to fight with Roy.

"I was kidding."

"I know." She didn't find the joke humorous.

"Just because he's nice doesn't mean he won't put you in jail if he finds out who you really are, Hannah." Roy, her best friend, forever her angel on her right shoulder, the voice of reason.

Her chest developed a dull ache. What if she walked away from burglarizing jewelry stores today? Never stealing another piece of precious stone again. Would she be able to have a relationship with someone like Jason if she left the life behind? Not necessarily him, but a genuinely trustworthy man with his life put together. A man who would support the woman he loved in every meaning of the word. A man who'd support her through thick and thin and if she screwed up, he wouldn't drown with her, he'd pick her up, brush her off, and hold her hand.

"Hannah." Roy plucked her from her reverie. "He can't be the man for you."

"I know." A sharp pang of regret stabbed Hannah. A first for her.

## 16

Jason shut down his work laptop and stretched his arms over his head. His back ached from being slouched for hours on end. He hadn't taken a break from writing a report on the detective team's next strategy in the jewelry thief case. That morning he'd approached Chief about hitting some local gyms to do some undercover work. Attempt to get a couple profiles started on women whose figures resembled their burglar's. Her shape was quite distinct. Chief gave permission for the research. Himself, Dean, and Tyler were allowed to scout the local gyms. Jason's theory included the fact their perp had to be in exceptional shape. Not only evident from her tight suit but she also had to be physically strong to get in and out of the stores as well as be able to break the glass on the display cases without the aid of a weapon. How she managed to do that without spilling blood suggested her gloves were constructed of a heavy duty material.

Hitting the gyms gave them some sort of action with regard to the case. The standstill bred angst among the detective team.

Jason snatched up his car keys for the drive home. He planned to stop at Hannah's and ask her to Dean's party on Saturday. He continued to pussy out calling her, instead deciding a face to face gave her less opportunity to turn him down. He'd recognized the imminent denial in her eyes when he asked her for a second date. Their overheated kiss did him in and he remained unfocused. The phantom sensations of her fingers gliding across his skin continued to haunt him. Hell, last night it startled him out of a deep sleep, which consisted of Hannah as the star of a fine dream. He'd been thoroughly disappointed to find himself alone. And even more depressing, his hand, not Hannah's, down his boxers.

Fifteen minutes later, Jason knocked on Hannah's apartment door. He stood in the hallway, his hands shoved into his suit pants, waiting. He pressed his ear to the solid steel structure. He didn't hear a television or footsteps. Dumbass. Like he'd be able to hear anything through that thick design. The door from across the hall swung open and a couple in their late sixties stepped out.

"Hello." The woman kindly greeted him.

"Hello, ma'am."

"If you're waiting for Hannah, she left an hour ago, honey." The woman closed the door behind them and locked it. "She's rarely home in the evenings."

Why would she not be home in the evenings? Her job description seemed like one that would be done during the day. Unless...

Was she dating someone else? Damn it. He didn't consider he might not be the only man to ask her out to dinner. Hannah's stunning looks and vibrant personality could have men constantly falling at her feet. Dating 101–make certain the woman you're courting isn't playing the field. This was a prime example of an enormous mistake when a man doesn't keep himself in the dating pool and his instincts on the opposite sex sharp.

The couple went to the elevators as he stood there like an idiot, staring at the closed door and the gold knocker, a lioness. When he heard the ding of the elevator arrival, he turned to leave. Hannah stepped off the elevator, dressed in a black wrap dress and black flats. Her fiery red hair piled high on her head in a messy do gave off the impression she'd carelessly pulled it up to get the tresses out of her way. She stole his breath. Jason pitched out a hand and braced himself on the wall to prevent from hitting his knees.

She stopped and said hello to her neighbors before she saw him. A small hiccup in her step that most people wouldn't have detected almost caused her to trip. What did that mean?

As she drew closer, his eyes bounced from her milky white cleavage that peeked from the V of her dress to her sharp blue eyes and back.

"Eyes up, buddy," she said, her voice low and husky. "You don't get to ogle the girls unless I give you permission."

"Sorry." His cheeks flushed hot. Damn it.

She pulled out a set of keys.

"Are you dating someone?" he blurted. He unsuccessfully tried to keep his eyes from her ample chest.

Her eyebrows knitted together. "No. Why do you ask?"

He motioned a finger at her outfit. "You're dressed like this and your neighbors said you're gone most evenings."

She grew in height as her jaw clenched. She placed a hand on her hip. "Are you spying on me?"

"No." He held up a hand. He didn't want to come across as creepy cop guy. "I came to ask you out again. To a get together this Saturday. A picnic of sorts. But you weren't here and the neighbors..."

He clamped his mouth shut, realizing nothing coming out sounded appropriate to a single woman, whose apartment he stood in front of, drilling her like a suspect.

Hannah shoved the key into the lock, swung open the door, and ushered him inside. "Let's not do this so my other neighbors get a show. I'm not exactly a soap opera fan."

Jason stepped into her place, feeling like a young boy reprimanded. Not a state he welcomed.

Hannah shut the door and spun on him. "First, don't you ever show up on my doorstep acting like some cop demanding answers about my social life again. We," she gestured between them, "are not a couple. We aren't even considered dating. 'Dating' constitutes more than one date. We have been on one. Singular. And the odds for a second night out are diminishing, buddy."

She pushed that finger dead center in his chest.

Man, she was beautiful when angry. Her eyes burned with fire. Her high cheekbones twitched while she gnashed her teeth. She was really pissed.

"You still haven't answered my question." He poked the bear again.

Her mouth fell open. "Did you not hear one word I just said?"

"I did."

"And you deemed it necessary to ignore me?"

"I decided it's necessary to get answers to my questions."

"Ugh." Hannah flung her hands up and stalked into the living room area. "I suppose this is what I get for going out with a cop, one time. Once. This is where I end up."

"Detective."

"Whatever."

She wheeled around and leaned against the back of the large plush sofa, her arms propping her up, shoving her breasts outward. How the hell was he not supposed to stare? Talk about testing a man. "No, I'm not dating, speed dating, playing the field, or have a friend with benefits, with anyone. Including you. There, now get out."

"Wait," he stammered. Shit, he went about this all wrong. "Why? Wait. You can't just throw me out."

"The hell I can't." She pointed to the door. "Out."

"I'm not a dog, Hannah."

She grinned, the look more sinister than friendly.

"You're right. I'm sorry. Come here," she said, her tone soothing.

Jason approached her.

Her eyes glittered. "You sure you're not a puppy?"

Damn it. Furious and without thinking, he tackled her backward, both tumbling over the sofa, bouncing off the cushions, and hitting the floor with a thud. Jason landed on top of her, staring down into her beautiful eyes.

"Get. Off. Me." She pushed at his body.

He couldn't resist, he leaned down and kissed her full berry lips. A small peck, another taste. He wouldn't let her go that easily. Couldn't allow her to throw him out on his ass without a chance at a second date. His approach showed his idiocy. Jason needed to correct his mistake or else regret his decision in trying to get to know this beautiful woman.

Her body relaxed underneath him as he kissed her again, this time deepening the connection. Her arms wound around his neck as he slid his right hand up to cup the back of her head. His tongue sought more, snaking out and demanding hers. She complied, their mouths in an erotic dance. Her floral scent engulfed him, luring him in. He couldn't get enough of her. She consumed his dreams at night and during the day crept into his psyche. For some inexplicable reason, this woman catapulted her way under his skin.

Slowly his body undulated. She moved with him. He wanted her. He wanted to be inside her. He wanted to worship every inch of her delectable body. He let himself go, his control perilously hung by a thin thread.

A loud grumble roared from Hannah's stomach.

Hannah busted out laughing as Jason pushed back to make certain an alien hadn't crawled out of her body.

"If you must know where I was this evening, I was going to get something to eat but the restaurant was booked and there was no place to sit at the bar. I came home to raid my fridge, but finding something edible is slim to none. I go out every night, as I have yet to develop the skill to cook for one. I'm single. It's not a breeze." Hannah pushed him away and stood, straightening her dress.

Jason crawled off the floor, adjusted his pants to try and mask his desperate erection that wanted to puncture his pants. "I haven't eaten, either. Let's go find something. I'm sure there's a pizza place around her somewhere."

"I don't eat garbage," she huffed.

"Great, you can have a rabbit salad while I hog down a slice loaded with every form of meat the place has in stock." He grabbed her hand and pulled her out the door. Date number two.

## 17

Hannah snorted, the water she just took a sip of going up her nostrils. She grabbed her paper napkin and coughed.

Jason smacked her back. "You okay, there?"

She shook her head and took in a deep breath. "You can't tell me those stories while I'm eating or taking a drink."

"But it's funny."

"It's hysterical, but bad for my health. I could have choked."

"I know the Heimlich. You'll be fine." He took a large bite of his weighed down slice of pizza.

"So what did you do after you uncuffed him from pole?"

"Had him dress and hauled him off to jail."

"While he still had strawberry sauce all over him?"

Jason lifted one shoulder indifferently. "Didn't care if he was suffering. He trespassed into his ex's house and went all stalker guy. Totally against the law. He didn't smell so great the next day appearing before the judge after a night sweating in lockup."

Hannah laughed so hard, she nearly fell off the stool. Jason reached over and snatched her around the waist, hauling her close. They sat in front of the large windows, eyeballing the crowd that littered the South Side while they ate their pizza. Jason had entertained her with tales about his days as a beat cop. Most of his stories were lighthearted, punctuating that the general public was full of some crazy characters. She had a notion he kept the harsh stuff locked away. She wondered if he'd venture into his detective world.

She probed. "Anything that crazy since moving to detective?"

"No. It's different." He finished off his pizza and took a long drag from his water.

She waited for him to elaborate but when he remained tight lipped, she chose not to pursue. For now. Or ever. She shouldn't be sitting next to Jason, no matter how attractive, amusing, and intelligent he was. She shouldn't welcome her relaxed state in his company. She shouldn't find him sexy and comfortable. She shouldn't find herself drawn to him.

"You never did answer my question. Will you come with me to the picnic on Saturday?" Jason proved he wouldn't be deterred.

"Jason, you're a great guy—"

He groaned in protest. "Don't even give me the 'nice guy, but it's me not you' line. That's bullshit. You're just as attracted to me as I am to you."

"Attraction and dating are two different items," she noted.

"You go out with someone you're attracted to. That's how it all starts. Generally, men don't ask out women they don't find appealing." His eyes were like laser beams, burning into her.

"True, but I'm just not at a point in my life that starting any form of relationship is a novel idea." No matter who she went out with, until she walked away from heisting jewelry stores and even beyond then, she'd put them at risk. She would blindside any man with her hidden secret if she got caught. Some might suggest that it was only a matter of time before the police caught up to her.

Jason stared at her, his sharp icy blue eyes bore into her as they narrowed. "Why are you trying to hide from me?"

She didn't know if Jason heard her sharp inhale, but the wind sure as hell left her lungs in an agonizing rush. A distinct pain shot through her chest. Her stomach cramped and churned. This is what happens when you get too close to an cop. They pick up on things, just like Roy warned. She went out with Jason twice and he already, unknowingly at that very moment, danced the line of figuring out she possessed a dark secret.

Time to nip this immediately. "Jason, I could never be an officer's girlfriend."

The moment his features dropped and his face took on a blank mask, she hated herself and the uninvited awareness of guilt that raced through her veins.

He swiped at his mouth with a napkin and stood abruptly. "Let me take you home."

The painstakingly silent car ride back to her apartment seemed to take hours, not minutes. She precisely hit a sore spot with Jason. Hannah had no clue that one comment would do the trick.

## 18

Jason lingered off to the side of the firepit in Dean's backyard. He worked on his third beer since he arrived. To say his mood remained sour wouldn't be accurate enough. Even the party surrounding him with loud music, singing, and laughing couldn't yank him out of his melancholy. Since Hannah doused him with a reality check, he had considered what she said. At his age, most cops were married with families. He hadn't been interested in settling down. He couldn't have cared less as long as he had the occasional tryst to quench his occasional sexual thirsts. After watching his LEO brothers get destroyed by women and loss, he knew he didn't want that life. He'd accepted and been all right with that decision. Until Hannah.

But what Hannah boldly said stung. Deep. And provoked too much dwelling. He wouldn't be able to find a woman who could handle his career choice. Inevitably leaving him in a lifetime of uncommitted relationships. Being married to a law enforcement officer burdened some spouses. Walking out the door every shift, not knowing if his brothers will show up on the doorstep to give her the most awful news a wife could ever receive—that her husband was killed in the line of duty. It took a special breed of woman to handle their chosen career and go on about their daily lives.

But he'd moved up, where he no longer drove the streets at night or went on calls for domestic cases. Those days ended with his promotion. His shifts did maintain long, grueling hours and he came home exhausted. He could never be in a relationship with Hannah and give her his full attention. She would always take a back seat to his job. He'd likely miss her birthdays and their anniversaries. He'd seen many men miss the birth of their children. But their ardent wives stuck by them. They understood their husbands' profession and commitment to their communities and upholding the law. For someone who'd never been privy to the life of a LEO, it would take a toll on her and she fully admitted truthfully she couldn't deal.

He should appreciate Hannah's brutal honesty. But he didn't. He hated that the one woman he connected with rejected him due to his career.

Jason watched Dean mosey by with a young woman under his arm. She wore short shorts on the warm, early fall day, an extra small tank top, and sandals. Her long black hair flowed down her back and she wore her makeup heavy. The type did nothing for him. She didn't compare to Hannah. Frazzled, gorgeous Hannah, who didn't care that a hair stuck out of place and wore minimal makeup to cover her porcelain skin that didn't need the enhancement.

Discontented, he downed the remainder of his beer and headed into the house to retrieve a replacement. Inside, he found his brothers gathered around the television watching the Pirates game.

Chief saddled up next to him. "What's going on, Campbell?"

He popped the lid off the longneck. "Nothing." He nodded to the TV. "Who's winning?"

"Pirates, six to four, bottom of the eighth."

"Nice."

"You've been quiet the past few days. Something happening I should know about?" Chief asked.

Generally, Chief didn't pry, but Jason understood where he came from. He'd been an angry bear prowling the precinct for days, biting at anyone who crossed his path. If he couldn't think properly on the job, he could essentially create havoc within the precinct and out in the field. It happened to both Dean and Nick. A brother's head that couldn't be all in the game was a dangerous partner to his brothers. "No."

"You're lying."

Jason did not favor Chief's psych couch. "Just dealing with some personal issues."

"Which are?"

"Women."

Chief scowled. "I thought you were single."

"Still am."

"And that's the issue?"

"Yep." He took another long inhale of his beer, allowing the cool taste to soothe his throat. Hopefully the alcohol would kick in soon.

Chief faced him, his man-in-charge facet in full force. "A cop's girlfriend, fiancée, wife is a special type, Campbell. You know that. Your father married one. Not many of those women exist. Yeah, we see the girls that Dean chases, but those aren't the women that can maintain a house, that can handle the long hours and anxiety when you walk out the door. The five of us? All single for a reason. Well, Dean's case is a bit extraordinary. Can't fault him for the path he's chosen." He slapped Jason on the back. "It's possible all five of our boneheads will end up old men gathered in a nursing home remembering the good ol' days with each other." He grew serious. "Don't think you have to find someone just to make certain you don't come home to an empty bed at night. The trade off isn't worth it. Ask Nick."

By trade off, Chief meant a woman who wasn't all in. A woman he might end up placing a ring on her finger and inevitably divorce, losing half of what he worked so hard to build. Jason glanced Nick's direction. His buddy sat on the sofa, immersed in the baseball game. Deep stress lines that never went away after his divorce etched across his forehead.

Jason downed his beer in a few long gulps, ready to lose himself in a night of drunken stupor. Dean traipsed by and went straight upstairs with a woman tucked under each arm. How the hell did his partner find a second one?

He should take on Dean's lifestyle. Keep himself sexually satisfied and a warm bed a couple nights a week, instead of waiting years and getting himself all moony over rejection.

\*\*\*

Two weeks later, Jason tidied up his desk after he changed into jeans and a black T-shirt. For a man who hadn't gone out on a date in such a long time, he now had his fifth in the past fourteen days. Yet not one woman held his interest.

Jason plugged away at the dates, hoping for some sort of connection or instant attraction. But at the end of the evening, he walked the women to their front door with a quick kiss on the cheek and said he'd call them. He hadn't phoned one of the women for a second night out.

Tonight the guys arranged their normal weekly get together that had taken a back seat in the past few months. Tyler planned to bring his childhood girlfriend. Apparently the two were an off and on thing for years.

When Jason strolled through the doors to the sports bar a half an hour later, he found his friends hovering by the pool table and Tyler with his arm around a pretty brunette.

As soon as he approached, Tyler did the introductions. "Jason, this is my girlfriend Kayla. Kayla, this is Jason Campbell."

"It's a pleasure, Kayla."

"It's nice to meet you, too. Tyler talks about you guys so much, it's finally nice to put faces to names." Kayla smiled brightly, her hazel eyes alight with palpable glee.

Tyler stiffened and reddened at his girlfriend's admission that he talked shop.

"Well, don't judge us by anything Tyler says. Dean *is* an asshole," Jason said, loud enough to grab his partner's attention.

"Hey." Dean jaunted over. "I resemble that remark. Tyler won't let go of his girl, probably afraid I'll swoop in." He winked at Kayla.

"You stay away from her," Tyler grumbled.

A tall, gorgeous blonde stepped up next to Kayla and handed her a glass of red wine.

"Jason, this is Danielle. Danielle, This is Jason." Tyler motioned between them.

Danielle, the blind date Tyler surmised would do Jason a world of good. She held out her finely manicured hand. Jason took her palm and shook gently, afraid of breaking her wrist. Her contact was weak and demure. In fact, scrutinizing her, she needed to eat a burger. Not that he had an issue with thin women, but she looked too skinny.

"Nice to meet you, Jason." Danielle gave him a once over.

"Likewise."

"Danielle works for my father," Tyler said.

Ah, so that's Tyler's game. Set up one of his LEO brothers with someone from his father's office, that way he wasn't the only one on the team with political connections. Cagey, and a waste of time for Jason.

Jason refused to be pulled into the legislature spectrum but he'd be polite to Danielle. After all, she couldn't be blamed for his zero interest in becoming a political minion. "What do you do for Senator O'Neill?"

"I'm one of his advisors." She expertly whipped out a business card.

How very intimate.

He took the card and shoved it into the back pocket of his jeans.

"Hey, you guys in for some pool?" Nick racked the balls.

"You both in?" Tyler asked him and Danielle.

Jason shrugged. "Sure."

"I'll watch, if you don't mind. I can't play." Danielle took a sip of her wine.

Kayla looped her arm through her friend's. "Neither can I. We'll watch together."

Fifteen minutes of horsing around and finally the guys split themselves into two teams. Nick and Dean partnered against Tyler and Jason.

Tyler continued to wander over to Kayla, the two clearly smitten with each other.

"How long have you known one another?" Jason asked as Tyler leaned over the pool table to take a shot.

Tyler sunk a stripe. "Since grade school. Both our parents are actively deep in the government. At a young age, it was voiced loud and clear our parents wanted us married."

No pressure.

"It's just dumb luck we happen to love each other. For the most part. Sometimes the family dynamic gets too overwhelming for us." Tyler sunk another stripe.

Jason was stunned by Tyler's admission. He never discussed his family or his personal life. The tension must be insurmountable for Tyler. To be the son of a senator, who held high expectations and aspirations, had to be burdensome.

"We're trying to work it out right now, but things have been rocky for the past year." Tyler took a shot and missed.

"Amateur," Dean ridiculed from across the table.

"I'm sorry to hear that." Jason sincerely meant it.

Tyler shrugged but the move didn't come across as irreverent as he probably meant. "It is what it is."

Dean went on a table clearing rampage.

"Tyler, are you hungry? We were going to order something to snack on." Kayla had an appetizer menu open with Danielle reading over her shoulder.

Jason glanced at his watch. "I could eat, if everyone wants to grab something."

"Dude, as soon as we kick your ass in this game we'll eat," Nick said. Dean pocketed the eight ball. Nick rolled his eyes. "Fine, we're ready."

Dean and Nick fist-bumped their win.

The girls grabbed their purses and Tyler rushed to the hostess to nab a table. They all strolled to the dining section. Jason held out a chair for Danielle and sat next to her. Tyler and Kayla settled down across from them and Dean and Nick on either side. A waitress approached and took their drink orders.

"Jason?"

He stiffened at the low, sultry voice.

"I think I've died and gone to heaven." Dean held his beer in mid air.

"Holy shit." Nick's eyes went wide as saucers.

Jason turned in his chair to find Hannah standing behind him, a bag in her hand. He gulped, his collar tightening. His body went hot. His jeans constricted in front as he drank her in.

She exuded sensuality. Dressed in faded jeans that fit a bit too large and hung low on her slim hips, a white button down v-neck shirt that clung to her curves, black flip flops with black painted toenails, and her hair cascading down her back, every man—taken or single—stared her direction. And he wanted to punch all the gawkers in the throat, including his two brothers, whose tongues might as well be hanging out of the sides of their mouths.

"Hi," she said. "I thought that was you I saw as I was picking up some food."

On their own accord, his legs propelled him out of his chair. "Hi."

Hannah slanted a side glance at Danielle, who blatantly scrutinized her. A distinct air of superiority crossed over Danielle's features. Hannah must have registered it, because she grew interested in her feet.

"Well, it was good seeing you." She gave a small, skittish smile and held up the restaurant to-go bag. "I have to get this to my friend."

"He?" Jealousy rankled him. She was taking care of another guy? He wanted to be the one she picked up food for.

He froze at that thought. Where the hell was his mind at? She deliberately rejected him, he couldn't allow himself to want her.

Hannah smiled affectionately. Again, the green-eyed monster growled. "He's got that condition where he's afraid to leave his apartment and go outside. He won't even step into the hallway of his building. I have to take care of him or else he'll starve."

Their first meeting clicked. "That's why you had a shopping cart full of food."

Hannah's eyes lit and her grin went wide at his perception. The look went straight to his gut. She was so beautiful and personable and his desire of her bewildered him.

"Guilty," she said.

Dean appeared at her side, holding out a hand. "Hello. I can't believe how rude my friend Jason is. We weren't formally introduced at the coffee shop. I'm Dean Rooney."

Hannah took his proffered hand. Jason caught she didn't possess a dainty greeting. She got in there and held her own with Dean. "Nice to officially meet you."

"Pleasure is mine. Would you like to join us?" Dean did not release her hand, caressing it with his thumb.

Jason swiped at his partner's limb and pulled Hannah to his side. "Stop flirting. She won't buy into your shit."

Hannah pointed to his partner. "True, I won't. But you sure do stroke a girl's ego, Dean."

"I aim to stroke."

"I bet you're an expert at it." Hannah playfully tapped Dean's chest.

"I do consider myself proficient."

"How long does it take for you to stroke yourself? And where do you like to stroke? Shower? Bed? Car?" She challenged, much to Dean's scandalized surprise.

Jason, Nick, and Tyler unsuccessfully choked back their laughter.

"Holy hell, I think I just fell in love," Nick said. "She totally dogged Dean."

Dean pegged her and grinned. "You. I like."

"Take a number, Dean."

"I will. If this one doesn't get his shit together and claim you first." Dean went back to his chair and planted himself, picked up his beer, and took a swig, his eyes never leaving Hannah.

Danielle stood. "I suppose I should leave."

Hannah stopped her with a gentle hand on the shoulder. "No, don't. I just came over to say hello. I was surprised to see Jason here, that's all. There's nothing for you to worry about."

Danielle huffed. "Clearly you have no clue how to read men. I have no chance competing against you."

"There's no contest."

"You're right. There's not. I was never in the game." Danielle wrenched her purse over her arm and fled the restaurant.

Hannah whirled on Jason, anger riddled her features. "What the hell did you do to her?"

"More like who the hell are you and what have you done to Jason?" Tyler asked, standing and following after his father's advisor.

"What does that mean?" Hannah's clipped question accompanied a frown.

"Means, dear Jason wouldn't give Danielle the time of day. But as soon as you come into the picture, he gets all possessive and flustered. Where have you been hiding her, partner?" Dean asked.

Jason glared at his friends. Fucking douche bags. They couldn't leave well enough alone. It was bad enough he made an ass out of himself in front of everyone, but they had to call him out on it?

Jason's blood boiled. He reeled on her, zeroing his anger and frustration on her. "There's nothing for her to worry about? Really, Hannah? You're going to play that game? Fine."

How dare she question him when she'd dismissed him. She had absolutely no right or say with his dates or what events took place on those dates. Or in his life, period. Jason had given her the opportunity to be the object and center of his nights but she viciously rebuffed him. Fuck her.

Jason stormed past her and out of the restaurant. He went straight to Danielle, who hovered by Tyler's Mercedes. Jason marched straight up to her, snagged her around the waist, leaned down and kissed her. No, he didn't full-out assault her mouth. The kiss was hard on the lips. One to prove to himself that he could be just as nonchalant as Hannah over a potential relationship. One that would shove her out of his head. One that would say *fuck you, Hannah.*

Except it didn't work.

Danielle pushed against his chest. "What the hell?"

"Sorry." Mortification slammed home. Jesus, what the hell was he thinking?

"Ordinarily I would have accepted that kiss. Except I know what you're doing and I won't be used to prove a point to yourself or another woman," Danielle snapped.

Jason rubbed the back of his neck. "You are absolutely right. I apologize. I am so sorry for disrespecting you."

She focused on something or someone behind him. He could easily guess. "I forgive you. I've been in the awful place where you are."

Jason didn't want to glimpse over his shoulder to a vehicle's squealing tires leaving the parking lot. He knew whose car barreled away from the restaurant.

"She's beautiful," Danielle said.

"She is." He couldn't agree more, but it didn't matter that he pined for Hannah. She stated her opinion loud and clear. "But she doesn't want me.

She can't handle my line of work and I can't be with someone who won't accept my career. Not that I asked for much. Only a date."

Danielle looked at him sympathetically. "I totally understand." She smiled beautifully, her stance losing its rigidness, and then gave him a blatant invitation. "Why don't you come back to my place?"

## 19

Hannah sobbed incredibly hard, her body convulsing with hiccups. Roy paced, a tattered mess, not knowing how to handle the situation. She lay on his sofa, crying into a plush pillow over a man she couldn't be in any sort of relationship with. She desperately wanted to climb into bed with Jason, make love to him, and wake next to him in the morning. A couple. A man she could treasure and build a life with. She could envision a future that consisted of the two of them in a weekly routine. Saturday yard sale browsing, Tuesday movie night, Wednesday restaurant dinner night, and Friday happy hour. But that scenario would never come to be. She boxed herself into a corner with her illegal activities.

How could she get out of the mess she created? How could she find a normal life for herself when her history provided a potential for so much personal destruction?

Roy sat down beside her, lifting her head and placing it in his lap. "Shhh. It's going to be all right."

"No it's not. He kissed another woman, Roy. He kissed her when I pushed him away because I won't have anything to do with him."

"He'll put you in jail. I couldn't bear to see you behind bars," Roy said. "'You're too good of a person. And I'd never survive without you."

"I deserve to be in jail."

"Do I deserve to be in jail? If you get caught, I'll have a one-way ticket along with you."

"No!" She'd be devastated and heartbroken if Roy ever took blame for her criminal activities. "But I do. I'm the mastermind. I deserve to spend time behind bars."

Roy bolted up. "You shut up. Don't you ever utter those words again. I won't have it. You don't deserve the life you've been handed. You had shit parents who forced you to find a way to survive."

"I could have found another way." She buried her head into the pillows.

"How? How could you come up with fifty thousand dollars on a week's timeline? Twenty-five thousand on three days' notice? Sixty thousand in five days? That's what you were dealt with time and again, or else you end up with broken limbs, or worse, six feet under. You've done what's necessary to survive." Roy's tone turned soft and sympathetic.

"What's my excuse for continuing down the path?" She had none. Her parents didn't owe any money, that she knew of. She clung to the theory the debt collectors would return and find her. Like a lifeline, she held tight and refused to release her tight grip on surviving by any means necessary. Only one other theory existed. "Greed."

"I'll agree, but I also understand why you've allowed the money to become the driving force of your life. You've never had any. You've never lived comfortably. You grew up dirt poor, sometimes going days without food when your parents inevitably spent their money on drugs and booze and gambling. You watched your parents owe money they never had to people who always came collecting." Roy's impassioned speech nailed her in the gut. He grew agitated. She blinked up at him, hurt. "You could stop any time and not pay your parents' debt. The mob will eventually kill your parents when they realize your bank account has dried up. But you continue to play. You've become addicted to the game. All aspects of it. Do you need that luxury car or to shop every other day for clothes or go out to dinner nightly or join the best gym in town? Those are your real reasons. This has been in your hands for years to right and you've maintained the inevitable collision course with law enforcement. You only have you to blame now. No matter how much I try to convince you to walk away, you always come back with the same excuse—your parents. I've been stupid and blind enough to follow you anywhere and accept your justification."

He stormed to his bedroom and slammed the door shut.

Great, not only did she manage to destroy any semblance of a possible relationship with Jason, she pissed off her best friend. Who knew she'd be batting a thousand in a game she despised.

Roy had valid points, she could walk away from her outlaw lifestyle. Yes, the money played a critical part in her mindset, but she couldn't let go of the fear instilled in her by the loan sharks.

Hannah pulled herself upright and swiped angrily at her tear-stained face. She had enough. For as long as she could remember, her life had been affected by others. She spent day after day looking over her shoulder, sustaining a direction she loathed. How badly did she wish to live a normal life? Oh, she masked her hatred of her life well. But every night, before she fell asleep, *what ifs* riddled her thoughts.

Those *what ifs* started to take over and roar like a pissed off lion, causing her to question her decisions, make her feel trapped, and to long for more.

Hannah grabbed her car keys, locked the door on her way out, and decided to head back to her place to wallow in self-pity and vodka.

\*\*\*

How Hannah ended up in Jason's driveway, she didn't quite know. But she sat there, car idling, headlights off. She glanced at the dashboard clock. One in the morning. She never planned to use Jason's address, which she stole from Roy's jotted down notes a couple weeks ago. Apparently her best friend did some virtual investigating on her crush.

Crush didn't accurately describe her devastation. What word would best depict her heartache?

A knock on her car window scared the shit out of her, causing her to squeak and jump. Jason's hard, icy stare seared her. He dressed in nothing but a pair of jeans, unbuttoned, showing off a lovely V-shape and that delicious notch from a religious workout regimen. A sexy line of hair from below his belly button that disappeared into his pants taunted her.

He opened her car door, yanked her out, and crashed his mouth onto hers in a scorching kiss. Jason pushed her against her car, ground his body against hers, as they inhaled each other. They were frenzied in their kiss and she'd be bruised tomorrow with the force he used. But she loved it. She wanted him. She wanted him close, his body against hers. She wanted him naked, his warmth heating her from the inside out.

Jason pulled back. "What are you doing here?"

"Did you sleep with her?"

He shook his head. "I need you."

Jason speedily shut off and locked her car, picked her up, wrapping her legs around his waist. "You're coming to bed with me and staying the night."

"Are you asking?"

"Fuck no. I've had it with this shit, Hannah." He took her mouth in another blazing kiss as he carried her inside, kicking the door shut behind them.

She didn't pay attention to the layout of the house as her hands hungrily wandered his smooth back and chest. She didn't care as long as he held her, kissed her. Jason carried her, with seemingly no exertion, upstairs to a bedroom. He cast her onto a large bed and immediately covered her with his big body, his mouth devouring hers. His musky, masculine scent blanketed her, pulling her into his thrall. She scored him with her nails down his back, wanting him closer.

Hannah pushed at his jeans, over his hips. Jason's hands roamed her body frantically. He popped the button on her jeans, stood, and hurled her flip flops out of the way before he pulled her jeans down her legs. She hadn't worn panties. Something she'd gotten used to doing a few years ago when she couldn't afford to replace her threadbare ones.

"Jesus," he breathed.

Seductively, she spread her legs for him and slipped her hands down her stomach to her tiny nub. She slowly massaged herself with a come-hither stare, her back arching over the need for something only Jason could provide.

She watched Jason shed his jeans in one fluid movement, his monster of an erection jutting out, pointing directly at her. Apparently he also preferred commando. Nice.

Jason palmed himself, languidly stroking as he intently watched her.

"Take off your shirt and bra." His voice was rough and commanding.

No hesitation on her part. Hannah hastily removed the rest of her clothing.

"I don't have condoms," he said.

"I'm on the pill."

"I'm clean."

"I need you." Her body was desperate and hot.

Jason leapt on top of her and in one swift movement, he impaled her. She screamed out in shock and pleasure.

Jason stilled, his features contorting in a masculine surge of ecstasy as he breathed out, trying to gain control. "Fuck."

When her body acclimated to his girth, she ground her hips, pleading for him to move. He obliged, pulling almost completely out and then pushing in to the hilt. He leaned down, sucked and laved at her nipples, inhaling as much of her breast as he could. This is what she craved from him—his want and hunger for her. She accepted the connection, safety, and desire. Warmth shrouded her. Too long she'd gone without any semblance of a physical and emotional connection to a man. Too long she'd been alone. If this only lasted one night, she'd take whatever she could and tuck it away for future memories to live off of.

Their bodies moved in perfect symmetry. His moans and her soft whispers of encouragement filled the room, the potent scent of sex swirled in the air. Her body climbed as he hit her womb with each thrust. His five o'clock shadow that grazed her neck, collar bone, and breasts sent her sensitized skin into overdrive. Her release hit suddenly, washing over her, her body bowing as a scream escaped and her fingers dug into his firm ass.

Jason's hips jack-hammered into her body, his grunts increasing, his mouth taking hers again in a demanding kiss. At that moment, she'd give him anything he asked of her. He broke from the kiss and his body went rigid, a bellow bubbling from within him when his body released inside her.

Their chests heaved as they tried to take air into their lungs. Jason kissed her tenderly on the lips as he rolled them onto their sides, his body still connected to hers. He brushed her hair back and kissed her again, their gazes locked into each other. She studied his incredibly handsome, clean cut features, realizing she was in more trouble than she could have predicted. Hannah was falling in love with a cop.

## 20

Jason stirred from a peaceful sleep, warm and comfortable, wrapped around the softest body he had the pleasure of lying against. He blinked his eyes open, his head resting above Hannah's, her red hair splayed wildly over the white pillow and her face. Carefully, he pushed her locks aside to admire her beautiful features. Magnificent didn't cover what he saw. He slid his hand around her flat stomach and drew light circles over her satin skin. His body went on instant alert, wanting back inside her.

The morning after sleeping with this woman, peace enveloped him, like something clicked into place. He didn't feel the need to get up, shower, and leave. Instead he wanted to stay in bed all day with her and figure out all the ways her body responded to him. He could envision waking to her every morning. How comforting would it be to have her at home waiting for him every night? To not walk into a dark, empty house with no life behind its walls. Alternately, Hannah would be there, giving his home a glow and spirit.

Hannah twitched awake. Jason chuckled and kissed the side of her neck. "Mornin'."

She stretched like a lazy kitten, flaunting her large breasts. "Good morning."

He traced a light finger over the swell of her perfect breasts. They were more than a handful and he could spend hours worshiping them, and never grow tired of the task. Jason leaned down and kissed her lips. "Hungry?"

"Not for food."

Not one to pass up a golden opportunity, he pushed her onto her back and slid into her wet core. Either she woke primed for him or remnants from the early morning sexcapades helped a smooth entrance.

"God, you feel so good." He closed his eyes, savoring the sensitivity.

Hannah's glassy eyes rolled as she squirmed beneath him. "Hard, Jason. I want it hard."

"Can you handle it?" he challenged.

"I can handle anything you throw at me. Can you handle me?"

"Oh, babe, you have no idea." He slammed home, lifting her hips to grind deeper. Her fluids slid down him, his body shuttering as tingles swept over his sensitized skin. It was so erotic and sexy as fuck. Wet slaps of their bodies fusing together filled the room. Hannah grabbed his thighs and braced herself. She marked him and he loved it. He wanted her to tag him. Score him with her nails so each time he moved, whether at work, at the gym, or cutting grass, he'd be reminded where the sting originated and be pulled back to this moment. Hell, Jason wanted to claim her. Never in his life had he wanted a woman badly enough to entertain such thoughts. Hannah had his mind spinning in uncharted territory.

They both came together, him spilling his seed deep inside her, her coating him with her pleasure. This woman could own him, Jason was so damn wrapped up in her.

\*\*\*

Hannah gently glided a washcloth over Jason's chest as the hot stream washed away their sweat and sex. Her dainty hands left not an inch of his body unclean.

"We don't know anything about each other," she said. "Last night and this morning could be a mistake."

He captured her wet form around the waist and pulled her flush against him. "I refuse to buy into that. I know you're aware of what we have, Hannah. I've never been so damn entranced by a woman. All I think about is you. All I want is you. We'll get to know each other as time goes on. What I do know is that I can't stand this pushing away game you continuously play. And the nitwit that I am, accepting it and convincing myself that not having you is for the best. This awful back and forth stops now."

Jason spun her and flattened her against the shower stall wall, surprised to find a tattoo on her lower back. A fancy H. His thumb skimmed over the design. "H for Hannah."

She giggled like a school girl. "No, see the curves in the design? It's the sign for Pisces. My sign."

He loved it. Jason hands wandered down the sides of her body, palming the side swell of her breast, her hourglass shape, her toned thighs. He hiked up her left leg, entered her from behind, and ran his tongue up her neck and bit her lobe. He whispered, "Quit pushing me away. I'm not going anywhere."

She grunted as he relentlessly pounded into her slick body. He clinched her hands and pinned them above her head, entwining their fingers.

"Oh, God." Her head fell back into his chest, her sopping hair clinging to his body.

"Do you like that?" He ground his pelvis deeper. "Does my girl like to be tied up? I'd love to cuff you to my bed so you never leave."

Hannah exploded, screaming out as her body trembled and pulled him in to her core. His release came so hard and sudden, black spots blinded him for a moment.

Jason never had so much sex within a twelve hour period. He didn't know his body could. Even in his early twenties, he never performed so heartily. But with Hannah, he just wanted to become a part of her and never leave. He seemed to have an endless hard on in her presence.

He leaned down and lightly sucked on her neck. A shiver shook her body. "I think I'm falling for you, Hannah."

She laughed nervously and bit her bottom lip. "Think? You damn well better be, considering how we've spent the past few hours."

Yep, definitely falling for her.

## 21

Hannah sat on the kitchen barstool in Jason's large home and inspected her surroundings. Obviously his mother chose what sparse decorations hung on the walls or displayed on the tables. Family pictures placed in random spots were the only sign of any attempt to bring life to the house. She noted the humble dwelling could benefit from a womanly touch.

Jason handed her a cup of hot coffee and propped himself on the counter, his hands wrapped around his own mug, elbows resting on the gray marble, to get close to her.

"Ask me anything," he said. "You're concerned about not knowing each other. Let's check off some boxes now."

She stared into his mesmerizing eyes, not knowing what to ask or even if she wanted to question him. She was afraid of his answers but even more frightened of what he would quiz her.

"Later." She chose to delay the impending inquiry.

He grinned and smiled benignly. "All right. Since you're going the chicken route, I'll start. Where would you like to go to eat? Or do you want to order in? I'm starved."

"I'm more a plain Jane. Meat and potatoes. Italian here and there."

"A woman after my own heart." He took a sip of his coffee. "Movie? In or out?"

"In."

"Popcorn?"

"The more butter the better."

He laughed, the sound carefree and jubilant. "Chick flick, action, or drama?"

"Definitely no horror, don't we have enough of that in real life?" She had never gone into a deep analysis as to what type of movie she preferred. She didn't frequent theaters. She favored paperback novels.

"Oh lord, you're one of those romance movie buffs, aren't you? I would not peg that in you." The mirth in his eyes twinkled.

A palpable wave of sadness consumed her. How was she going to pull a relationship off? She couldn't walk away from Jason now even if she wanted to. First, he would come after her and she knew it. Second, she didn't have the will to step away. He made her happy. Light swathed her, as if the potential of what might come tomorrow didn't matter. He made her feel safe. His aura so vivacious and masculine, even without laying one finger on her, he surrounded her.

What if Jason could protect her from any possible future visits from her parents' dealers? He held a badge. He was the law. If she abandoned jewelry store heists this very second, the possibility of being caught grew slim with each passing day. This could work. It had to. With Jason, she envisioned a future. A future filled with mornings just like today. Saturday nights curled up on the sofa watching a rented movie or binge watching a TV series instead of casing a jewelry store. Tears filled her eyes at all the wonderful possibilities and the potential for heartbreaking loss.

"Hey." Jason came around the island and wrapped her in his arms. "What's wrong? Don't tell me you're already having doubts. Don't we have to fight, or something, first?"

She embraced him, holding tightly to his white T-shirt. She inhaled his scent, committing it to memory. She didn't know what fate had in store for her but she'd cherish this time as long as she could.

"Nothing's wrong." Hannah buried her head into his chest to hide her visible qualms.

"You're crying."

"I'm not crying." She wiped her nose on his tee.

"Nice." He lifted her chin to peer into her eyes. "You can tell me anything. No matter what is on your mind or what you're worried about. I'm here."

With that assurance, Jason shoved the knife into her heart.

## 22

Jason surveyed the close up photos of the jewelry thief. Chief called in a favor to a task force member who performed wonders with video surveillance images and managed to get zoomed-in pictures. The picture didn't give them any clues. No skin or hair color, no scars or tattoos, or eye color. Something familiar about the photo did stick out to him but remained unclear.

"Told you she was hot." Dean flopped down in the chair next to him in the conference room. With his finger, he outlined the silhouetted shape of their perp.

"We still don't have anything on her." Jason pulled it out of his partner's paws.

"She's gone quiet." Chief walked into the room, lobbing a folder into the center of the table. "Which means she's either moved to another city or doesn't need the money."

Tyler snatched the folder and pulled out the contents. More close up photos from each robbery.

"Speaking of hot," Dean said. "How's Red?"

Jason punched his partner in the arm. "None of your business."

"You're dating her?" Tyler asked, his tone not kind. "You know I had to apologize to my father and her father over you."

"I'm sorry, man." He'd apologized too many times to count, but Tyler refused to let the screw-up drop. Every opportunity, Tyler reminded him that he offended Danielle. The kid really needed to learn to lighten up and don't sweat the small shit. Not that his actions toward Danielle should be considered a brush off. But he didn't possess the power to go back in time and fix mistakes.

"You should be. You never should have agreed to the date if you had another woman," Tyler mumbled.

"I wasn't dating Hannah at the time and you're beating a dead horse." Jason grew irritated.

"So you *are* a couple now?" Dean probed.

What did Jason call them? They hadn't set any firm relationship status. Over the past two months they spent as much time with each other as his job allowed. When he knew he'd be heading home, he'd call Hannah and ask if she wanted to join him. She always said yes and met him at his house. He even gave her a key to let herself inside so she didn't have to wait in her car in case he got delayed.

Jason busied himself with the written report on the images. "I suppose."

Nick scoffed as he entered the room, Styrofoam cup in hand. "What does that mean?"

"How about we address Campbell's love life during the soap opera weekly review?" Chief snapped. He pointed at the white board. "Focus."

"If she's quiet or left, what do you suggest?" Tyler asked.

"We need to go over all the information we have. Go back to the businesses and see if they remember anything. An irate customer, a woman browsing who never bought anything, a man who seemed a bit odd, on the assumption she is working with someone. Maybe the stores have remembered something since we've last talked to them. Anything. Go over every detail we have on the case. There's something we're missing." Chief nodded to the best picture they had of her. The one Jason had been studying. "I can't imagine this woman will walk away from this. I think it's impossible at this point."

"Why not?" Dean asked. "She didn't want to actually rob the stores. There's only one reason why people truly get into robbing banks, convenient stores, jewelry stores. Money." He held up the photo. "There is no way this woman, who could probably do any job she wished, would sit up one day and say I want to steal diamonds. Which means, she's desperate."

"Which makes her dangerous," Chief said.

"True. But if she has gone off the grid, whatever she needed the money for is no longer plaguing her. Whether it's her mortgage, credit card debt, spousal support, car payments, or to feed her kids, she's okay right now. She found a way out of her situation and doesn't have to live a life of crime." Dean set the photo down.

"Guilt got to her?" Nick suggested.

"A guilty conscience doesn't get her out of being brought to justice," Tyler said.

Dean's voice raised, exasperated. "All I'm saying is that we might be running in circles on this one. We can go over all the evidence again and again and drive ourselves insane, but at what cost? We're spending all our time and resources on this one case and have nothing."

Chief glared Dean's way. "We aren't shelving this case. She's stolen hundreds of thousands of dollars in diamonds. She needs brought in. Tyler and Nick, I want you two to get back in touch with

McIntyre's and see if they're willing to cooperate yet. I want that store watched. I don't suspect for one minute she's finished. Whatever her reasons." He pegged the board. "She's in too deep. She won't be able to just walk away."

## 23

Hannah sat at Roy's computer, cursing. Filling out online job applications sucked.

"Where have you been lately? You haven't come around much. Are you angry with me? Have you been home?" Roy entered the small living room area with a sandwich in hand. He pulled up a stool next to her, hovering over shoulder.

"Nope, I'm not angry and no, I haven't been home." She hated keeping secrets from him, but he wouldn't understand.

"You going to tell me where you've been?" He took a large bite of his meal. "Don't tell me you're casing McIntyre's even after I told you to nix the project."

Hannah glared at him. "You know it's rude to talk with your mouth full. Pig."

"Sorry," he mumbled around his food. "What are you doing?"

"Applying for jobs." She clicked the agreement box for another online application. "I don't qualify for anything."

She grappled with her shame. An occurrence each time her lack of education presented itself. She never got her high school diploma. With all she went through—pounding music seven nights a week, parents who would knock on death's door from constant overdoses; drug deals, screaming battles with each other—she couldn't concentrate on her school work, pass tests, and had missed too many days. When she found out she wouldn't graduate, she caved to the pressure of living amid her parents' lifestyle, figuring what was the point of continuing another year. She wished she'd been mentally stronger at that time to plug out another year and earn her diploma. Why she never bothered obtaining a GED, she could easily answer. She hadn't needed one until now.

"What jobs are you applying for. CEO of the Heinz Corporation is taken." Roy rummaged through the stack of papers on his coffee table and pulled out a notepad for her to write on. "And why are you job hunting?"

"I'm going straight."

"Didn't know you swung the other way."

"Funny. I'm done breaking into jewelry stores." She scribbled down the name and phone number of the first two jobs and stores she applied to.

"Are you serious?" Hope streamed from every pore of his thin body. Roy constantly worried over her, to the point where she had to keep a cell phone line open during her heists, just in case. What he would do to help her, she didn't know. If her life was in danger, she didn't think even that garnered enough motivation to leave his apartment to save her. But she indulged him.

"Yeah."

"Why?"

She went to respond but clamped her mouth shut. How did she answer him? What was the truth? Was she trying to straighten herself in the interest of living a normal life? Or having a relationship with Jason? Yes and yes. But could she admit that to Roy? And fully to herself.

"Why?" he pressed.

"Jason." She clicked the submit tab to apply for a department store jewelry section position. Ironic. How she would explain a new job to Jason, she didn't know. She'd cross that bridge when necessary.

Roy jumped up. "Damn it, Hannah!"

"I'm in love with him."

He went still. "What?"

"I've fallen in love with him." She swiveled the computer chair to face him. "I couldn't help it. I tried, I really tried not to. But no matter how much I turned him away, we couldn't stay away from each other. There's something between us that I can't explain. He's everything I could ever want in a partner. He's kind, caring, smart, funny, and he's terrific in bed."

"Oh for God's sake, I don't need to know about that."

"He gives me hope for a future." She truly meant it.

Whatever inflection she used, it caused Roy's features to soften. He sat down next to her and took her hands into his. "What if he finds out what you've done? Will he still be able to love you?"

She'd asked herself that hundreds of times since she started sleeping with Jason. Dreams of Jason cuffing her and hauling her into the back of a squad car or confronting her with evidence of her heists, haunted her. All ending with Jason's reaction of betrayal, turning his back on her. She startled out of her sleep every single night. If that dream ever came to fruition, it would, in fact, be her worst nightmare.

"Can you be sure he'll love you if he finds out you're compromising his oath he took to uphold the law?"

The million dollar question Hannah prayed she never found out the answer to.

## 24

Jason led Hannah into his parents' home. He placed a hand on the small of her back. "Mom."

His mother rushed down the hall from the kitchen area, taking off her apron. "Jason, I didn't know you were coming." His mom glanced from him to Hannah and beamed. "Hannah."

"Sorry, are you busy?" He knew well enough that his doting mother would welcome him any time, especially with Hannah in tow.

Jason had finally resolved to bring Hannah home for a surprise introduction to his parents. He already knew where his mom stood on finding a girlfriend. He only hoped his mother held herself in check with her inevitable excitement. This could be a potential mistake. He didn't want his mom's exuberance to frighten Hannah.

"Absolutely not for my son. I'm finishing up some potato salad to go with dinner. Are you staying? Your father has the grill heated and is about to start steaks."

"Sure." He helped Hannah out of her fleece. "We could eat."

Hannah sniggered, a sound he loved coming from her. "He's always hungry."

His mom gave him a kiss on the cheek, took Hannah's hand and led her down the hall, toward the back door. "Let me introduce you to Jason's father."

"The grill master?" Hannah teased.

"Oh honey, you call him that and he'll become your new best friend."

Jason followed behind his mother and Hannah, grinning like a clown. His mom fired a glance over her shoulder and winked. Code for she approved. He shoved his hands into his suit pants pockets, his heart soaring. He'd fallen in love and his mom liked his choice.

\*\*\*

Jason changed his mind. He concluded his mother's acceptance of Hannah was bad. Very, very bad. They finished dinner and dessert and now the topic of conversion centered around him. For some awful reason, his parents deemed it necessary to tell Hannah every embarrassing story they possessed in their arsenal—including his father, which shocked the hell out of him. They held nothing back. Like when he and Dean played a prank on an unamused Chief, and in retaliation, punished them by commanding them to wear dry-erase boards all week. The catch? Their LEO brothers could write whatever they wanted on the boards. Who knew Nick could draw?

Stories of how he refused to be potty trained, or his superhero obsession phase, or snow boots all year round phase.

"All right, all right. Can we please stop giving my girlfriend comedy material? She doesn't need it, trust me." Jason cleared the dessert plates from the dining room table and returned with cups of coffee for everyone.

"But the stories are so good," Hannah protested.

"I'm sure Hannah has her own tales." His father grinned from ear to ear. Dad really liked Hannah. As soon as the words grill master left her lips, the man swooned. Mom knew his dad all too well.

Hannah paled and her eyes went wide for a brief moment before she caught and composed herself. His father's smile fell, the former career officer discerning her instantaneous mask.

Jason grabbed her hand and kissed the back of it. "You can tell them. They don't judge."

His mom's face went serious, growing concerned and understanding dawning. His dad went into what Jason referred to as "cop mode", ready to assess the situation.

"No, they don't need to hear about my sordid life story." Hannah fiddled with a napkin and gave a small, uncomfortable laugh.

His nurturing mother reached across the cherry wood dining room table and took her other hand. "Not if you don't want to, honey. Just understand, Mr. Campbell worked over thirty years as an officer. He's seen and dealt with it all. Nothing you ever wish to confess would shock us."

Hannah smiled tightly. "Thanks."

But she remained silent, refusing to divulge anything about her childhood. Not even the few details he knew. At that moment, it occurred to Jason he knew very little about her after dating her for just over two months. Only basic information and the short story about her parents and her friend who suffers from agoraphobia. But no intimate memories. Not even names. Her job hours seemed to coincide with his schedule, yet she never discussed her work day. She confessed nothing. Hannah kept herself a closed book.

Jason stiffened. Hannah may be sleeping in his bed nightly but he knew next to nothing about her. Realization that he never slept at her apartment hit him. He'd only ever stepped inside a few feet for a couple minutes, tops.

A barrage of questions assailed him. Why did she refuse to let him get to know her? Was it a result of her upbringing and she used it as a self-preservation mechanism? Was her motive to move along, having no intention of staying with him? What was she hiding or hiding from?

Fucking hell. He couldn't believe he'd been so drawn and obsessed with her that he overlooked getting to know her history.

Resolve to fix that tonight took hold and choked him. Why had it taken him so long to realize this? Because he's a fool who stupidly fell in love too quickly without thinking. Not that he didn't trust Hannah. He did, unequivocally. But he needed her to understand that she could come to him for anything, and she needed to start talking about her life secrets. He didn't like the perception of being left in the dark.

## 25

"Aren't we going back to your house?" Hannah was confused when he pulled his car into the parking lot of her apartment building. Did he not want her to spend the night? Did she say something to upset him or his parents? Did Jason's parents not like her? They seemed to. Did she misread the entire evening?

Her mind quickly ran through the conversations. Nope, couldn't come up with anything. She twisted the lightweight sweater she'd taken off in her hands.

"Just thought spending the night at your place would be a nice change." He narrowed his eyes her direction as he shut off the car engine. "If that's all right with you?"

This was a test. A challenge. Something happened. Something was up. What was going on? She had to play this carefully.

"Sure." She shrugged. "I don't have food. Or really anything to drink. Only stuff to make protein shakes."

"A protein shake in the morning is perfect."

"Oh, I do have coffee."

"Excellent." He opened up his door and climbed out.

She remained seated, baffled. His tone seemed almost confrontational.

Jason opened her door and held out a hand, helping her out of his sedan. He wrapped his hand around her waist and pulled her into his side, leaning down and kissing the top of her head. "I enjoyed tonight. My parents adore you."

She didn't understand the change of routine but if something concerned Jason to the point where he determined to take this route, she would go along. For now. She smiled up at him. "I like them, too. They're so kind and your father is one funny man."

Jason grinned. "He is."

They took the slow elevator to her apartment. She did a mental assessment of her condo for anything damning scattered about. When they walked through the door, she seemed fairly certain the black hip bag, diamonds, head mask, and money she had in the apartment were locked away in the chest located at the bottom of her bed or in her closet, which there'd be no reason for him to root through. She needed to transfer those belongings to Roy's apartment, where she stored the remainder of her job accessories.

Jason shut the door behind them and clicked the deadbolt into place. He slid out of his jacket. "Can I have a tour?"

"Sure." Her eyes searched his, not quite comprehending what was happening. He gave off an uncomfortable oddness. He seemed hard-lined and ready for a fight.

"Is everything all right?" She heard her own voice waver. She loathed the naked exposure of her insecurity with regard to him. "You aren't acting like yourself, Jason. You're sort of frightening me."

Not necessarily true, but he was making her jittery.

He unbuttoned the top of his white Oxford, guilt replacing his grievance. "I'm sorry. I got myself worked up at my parents."

"Over what?"

"It occurred to me I know nothing about you. You aren't very forthcoming." He approached her, slipped his hands into the back pockets of her jeans, and pulled her tight against him.

She wiggled away from him and escaped to her large apartment windows. The city skyline lit brightly from the buildings and baseball stadium. She placed her cheek against the cool glass, tears threatening. "I'm afraid you won't like what you hear. That you'll leave. That I won't be good enough for you."

She knew when he approached her, the heat from his body flooding her, like always. He placed gentle hands on her shoulders and spun her to face him. "How could you say that? Have I given you any inkling that I'm that type of man?"

"It's happened before. Not often. I haven't had that many boyfriends."

She heard a small growl burble up from his chest.

"Did you just growl?"

"Don't want to hear about you and other men, baby."

"Sorry." She laid her head on his chest, trying to compose her conflicting emotions and dire thoughts. "Men hear about my past, my family, and decide that I'm not girlfriend or wife material. They find out I didn't graduate high school and it's like I told them I have the plague."

"You didn't graduate?" He pulled back, perplexed. He glanced at their surroundings—the large wall-mounted flat screen, the designer furniture, the view of the city, the pristine shine of the fixtures, and the fine art hanging over the fireplace.

"How could they possibly judge you on that, when you've accomplished this?" He motioned around them.

"They never get this far."

A slow smile crept up. "I like that."

She playfully punched him in the shoulder. "If you want to know something, ask. I don't spill about myself to anyone. I learned at a very young age to keep quiet. I learned to keep my head down and do what it took to survive from day to day. Most of the time that meant keeping to myself and only trusting myself. This will take time. If you give me that leeway and help me, I'll learn to open up to you. I want to, trust me I do. I just don't know how."

"I'll teach you." He lightly pecked her nose with a tender kiss. "I can be patient. I shouldn't have gone straight to worst case scenario and should have addressed my concerns. All you had to do was explain. I won't push, Hannah. I understand the life you led. I've seen it. I know what an amazing woman you have to be in order to have survived and pulled yourself out of that world."

But she hadn't, really. Minus the past couple of months, she remained in the illegal activities that riddled the world, only she chose a more sophisticated crime.

She didn't want to think about that right now. Jason had his arms around her and when he did, she forgot about the shady character she took on at times. Instead, she could be the wholesome girlfriend with him. She liked playing the part. She fooled those she came into contact with, trying to become someone else—a better version of herself. In this reality she created, a happy medium existed for her. She gave such a first-rate performance she even fooled herself.

Jason leaned down and nibbled at her lips. "Give me a tour and then let me take you to bed and ravish you."

"If you insist."

"Oh, I do."

How much did she like bossy Jason? Her legs went weak.

\*\*\*

Hannah's body relaxed, her muscles loosened, like gelatin. Her back to Jason's front, the large jetted tub fit them well. Her body soaked up the hot water.

Jason ran a bath sponge across her shoulder blades, down her chest, and over her breasts. Their legs bent and hooked together left her exposed to him. Which he took advantage and already make her orgasm twice. The dirty man.

He leaned down and pressed a kiss to her shoulder. "Will you marry me?"

What?

Did he...

What?

"What?"

"Will you marry me?" His life-changing question held no doubt. "I love you. I want this every day for the rest of our lives. I want to make a life with you. Will you marry me?"

She burst into tears, her heart aching and soaring simultaneously. She loved him to her core. Their courtship was spontaneous, quick. That didn't matter to her, she could declare with her whole heart Jason was the love of her life. But their relationship was based on a lie. An enormous lie. One that would destroy them. Yet she didn't want to tell him no. He was everything she ever wanted. Jason could and most likely would pull her out of the hell she couldn't rid herself of, the one her parents thrust her into. The purgatory she created for herself. She could see the name Mrs. Campbell on checks and address labels. Hannah Campbell.

"Yes," she blurted, flipping and propelling herself into his arms. She didn't give a shit what he didn't know. She didn't care they barely knew each other and had only been dating for a few months. At this moment, at this time, they belonged together. Screw everything else. She refused to allow anyone or anything to come between them, including her damn criminal ways.

Jason kissed her long and deep. "Let me take you to bed."

"I like that idea."

"And we'll never leave."

She chuckled. "You have to work in the morning."

"So do you, don't you?" He climbed out of the tub and held out a towel for her.

"About that." She stepped into the plush material and allowed Jason to carefully wrap her up. "I'm job hunting. I lost mine a few weeks ago."

Jason stopped for a slight second while pulling a towel down for himself. "Why didn't you tell me?"

"I thought I could find something right away. Turns out the job market is more difficult than I gave credit."

"What happened?" He towel dried his body. She drank up every taut muscle that towel touched.

She blotted her hair. "My position wasn't needed any longer. Seems the company got what they needed from me and no longer required my services."

A semblance of truth to the statement. Not a total lie, right?

"I'm sorry, honey."

"Actually, I'm happy to be out of that business. It means I can move forward. Which I am."

"With me," he said. "You can move in to my house to save money. We're officially engaged, so why not?"

Talk about fast and spur of the moment. Her Jason didn't mess around. Moving in with him was a huge step. Not that an engagement wasn't. She'd have many loose ends to tie up before she played house with him. She'd need to permanently get rid of the evidence in her apartment and make certain that in no way her now former life seeped into Jason's. Could she do it? Yeah, why not? She'd figure it out. Just like everything else in her life. "Okay."

"Okay?"

She nodded. "Yes."

Jason scooped her up into his arms and carried her to bedroom. "You've made me the happiest man alive, Hannah."

Hannah could entirely relate.

## 26

Jason grabbed his car keys off his desk and slipped his arms into his jacket.

"You joining us?" Dean asked.

"I want to get home to Hannah."

Dean raised a brow as Nick and Tyler approached.

"You're ditching our Friday night happy hour for your chick?" His partner held a hand to his chest, mocking him.

"Leave him alone, Dean," Tyler said.

His partner smirked. "Not likely."

Dean propped his ass on the corner of Jason's desk and crossed his arms over his chest. "This how it's gonna be? Now that you've got yourself a hot tamale at home, we're left out in the cold? Not that I blame you."

"No." Jason may as well come clean. They'd find out soon enough. "I have to go to the jewelry store."

Nick laughed and smacked his back. "In trouble already?"

"I have to buy her a ring."

Crickets. Each one of them went mute. An anomaly.

"You're going to ask her to marry you?" Tyler's expression was one of shock. "You just met. You don't know her."

"I already did and she said yes."

"What?" Dean's humor vanished. "Jason, we need to talk about this. I mean, she's a catch, that's for sure. And everything you've told us about her seems great, but you don't know her that well. You've known her for, what, a couple months?"

Was it only two and a half months? Those who didn't know them, would presume their courtship time lasted years, not a whirlwind timetable of less than three months. People, specifically women, went on and on about love at first sight. Jason and Hannah's meeting didn't fall into that category, but it had been a quick courting since their initial run in. There remained no doubt in his mind he wanted to spend the rest of his life with her. To make a home with Hannah. To start a family with her. Man, even the thought of her belly round, carrying his baby, took everything in his will power not to insist she stop taking her birth control.

Jason pulled his wallet out of the top drawer and shoved it in the inside pocket of his suit jacket. "Doesn't matter. She's the one I want. I can't imagine my life without her."

His brothers gaped at him.

"I'm headed to McIntyre's to choose a ring and pull double duty to see if we can get some sort of cooperation from them since they turned down Nick and Tyler, again. Anyone want to join me or am I in this alone?" He gave his brothers a choice to either support him or turn their backs on his life changing decision.

Dean's eyes practically reached the ceiling. "Does Hannah know how overdramatic you are? I should warn her."

The guys burst out in hysterics.

Nick shook his hand and shoulder bumped him. "Congrats, man. I'll join you."

He had to give it to Nick, despite his horribly failed marriage, he kept his opinion about unions to himself.

"Congratulations, Campbell," Tyler said. "I wish you all the best."

Dean stood and embraced him in a manly exchange. "Congrats, Jason. You deserve it."

"Thanks." Talk about a guilt trip for skipping their Friday routine. Leave it to his brothers to be supportive. Deep down he knew they would be. He couldn't bug out. He didn't want the tight-knit group to disband on the grounds that one of them fell for a woman. "I'll call Hannah and tell her I'll be late. She'll understand."

"Of course I will," a sexy voice said from behind them.

The guys spun and collectively gasped. Jason's mouth hit the floor. Hannah wore a red sheath dress that hung to her knees and a pair of nude flats. Jason mentally noted that he needed to petition her to wear heels. She's mentioned in passing she found it difficult to walk in anything but flats. He'd stop at the shoe store and surprise her with a pair and possibly convince her to wear them around the house, while naked.

That sultry dress clung to her every curve. Jason didn't know if he liked her wearing it out and about without him by her side.

She approached the group, her luscious hips swaying. "I just stopped by on my way to an interview. I got called to come in at the last second. I don't know when I'll be finished. I could have called but this is on my way and I have a few minutes to spare."

Jason's hands went straight to her hips. "You are stunning."

"Yeah, she is." Dean openly drooled over his fiancée.

Nick smacked his partner in the back of the head. "Man, he's engaged to her now. You can't do that."

Hannah wrapped her arms around his neck, pressing her ample chest into his body. Instantly his own body stirred. Damn it. He didn't want to sport an erection in front of his brothers. But with Hannah's arms wrapped securely around him, he couldn't control his body if he truly wanted to.

"Since I don't know what time I'll be back, go do whatever it is you guys do. I'll just go straight home."

"*Our* home, or your apartment?" he tested.

"Sorry," she said, contrite. "My apartment."

No matter how many times he corrected her in the past week, Jason couldn't get Hannah to refer to his house as *their* home. He understood. She hadn't entirely moved in yet and placed her feminine stamp on the house. Which he expressed she had full rein. He supposed that would take time for her to adjust to as well.

"I'll call when I'm on my way back home and you can meet me. We need to discuss finishing moving you in." He wasn't going to allow her to delay the inevitable. He wanted her under his roof, in his bed. None of this two separate homes stuff. "The guys will help."

A collective groan came from each one of his brothers.

She mocked him by saluting. "Yes, sir."

Dean took her by the hand and slyly maneuvered himself between them. "Hello, Hannah."

"Hello, Dean." She batted her lashes flirtatiously.

"Stop that." Jason didn't like Hannah and Dean's breezy rapport.

Dean wrapped his arms around her waist, leaned down and kissed her cheek. He didn't cross a line, his partner's game to get him riled up wouldn't work.

Hell, who was he kidding, it worked. Brilliantly.

"So, darling, when do I get to take you out and you can tell me what you see in this big twit?" Dean asked.

Hannah laughed and toyed with Dean's jacket lapels. "Anytime, Dean. But I must warn you. I doubt very much you'll be able to handle spending an evening out with me. You should bring backup. I may just put your badge in jeopardy."

Nick raised his hand. "I'm in."

"Me, too," Tyler said.

A clearing of the throat interrupted them. Chief approached the small group. "What the hell is going on?"

"Chief." Jason took Hannah from his partner and spun her to face his boss. "I want you to meet my fiancée, Hannah Lakely. Hannah, this is our chief."

Hannah held out a hand and smiled, her beautiful features lighting up the entire drab room. "Nice to meet you."

Chief shook her hand. "Likewise. Have we met before?"

"No." She shook her head, those long tendrils swinging with the motion. Jason caught himself entranced.

"You look familiar." Chief studied her, giving her a once over. Jason didn't like it. He protectively wrapped an arm around her waist and tucked her into his side.

"Really?" she asked, skeptical. "The red hair is kind of telling. I mean, it's usually the first thing most people focus on."

Her words came across as almost confrontational, but not quite. Challenging?

"Not the first thing I noticed," Dean muttered.

Nick punched Dean in the arm. "Knock it off."

Chief smiled, his eyes crinkling. "A redhead spitfire. Good lord, Campbell, you're in trouble."

Hannah cackled, her head falling back. "He really has no clue."

Chief let out a rare booming laugh, took Hannah by the shoulders, out from Jason's grasp, and led her away. Jason stood, wondering what the hell just happened?

"Let's talk." He shot an order over his shoulder. "She'll be fine with me, Campbell. You guys go hit happy hour."

Hannah glanced over her shoulder and gave him a thumbs up.

Dean slapped his back. "Dude, I don't think for one minute you'll be able to handle her."

"Not at all," Nick agreed.

"I think she scares me," Tyler said.

They all left the station poking fun at Jason, who was a bit worried about what Chief had in store for his girl.

## 27

Hannah tried to play it cool. She breathed in steadily, calming the nerves that wanted to take hold and make her squirm. She learned a long time ago how to remain collected, no matter the given situation.

She never should have come to the station. She managed to make herself forget what Jason and his partners did for a living could destroy her. She drowned herself in playing the perfect girlfriend, banishing Hannah the thief. When she'd left Jason's home for the interview, she convinced herself that stopping by the precinct to let her boyfriend know she would be late was something a good fiancée did. She had hummed to the music in the car. She'd been excited to unexpectedly surprise Jason. Her lapse in judgment due to the delusion she created a sweet as apple pie girlfriend.

When Jason's chief asked if they'd met, a switch in her brain clicked, she played too close to the fire. The man had laid eyes on her for all of a couple seconds and his law enforcement radar went up. The dress. It had to be. The material hugged her abundant curves. Normally she wore form hiding outfits. Boyfriend jeans, looser T-shirts. Nothing that could pinpoint her with a mere glance of an eye. But the red dress called to her and she just had to give in. If she could kick her own ass, she would.

Now came the acting job of a lifetime.

"Please have a seat, Miss Lakely." Chief pointed to the chair facing his massive desk, littered with paperwork and folders.

"Please, call me Hannah." She kept her tone polite and carefree.

His smile showed off his handsome features. His uniform conformed to his body, not able to hide the fact the man frequented a gym. His biceps strained against his dark blue short sleeve Chief of Police shirt. The color of the uniform enhanced the dark blue of his eyes. Tiny crow's feet added to his distinguished aura. Funny how on a woman, those lines aged her. On a good-looking man like the chief, they contributed to his enticement.

"Hannah, so you and Campbell are engaged." Chief leaned back in his chair and crossed his arms over his wide chest. "That's surprising considering I had no idea he was serious about anyone."

She gave her best dreamy innocence. "I'm just as shocked as you. We've only been dating a couple months. But when he asked, I knew that yes was the only answer."

Chief narrowed his eyes, studying her. She forced herself to remain still under the scrutiny. She recognized when her charms didn't work. On Jason's boss, he seemed to be immune. Not good. Not good at all.

"I see." His arm muscles twitched. "You do understand that being a law enforcement officer's wife is taxing? It takes a certain woman to stand by a man in our line of work. One who can handle her spouse leaving the house for his shift and not drive herself insane with worry." He became pensive, as if having first-hand knowledge.

She sagged a bit, an effort to appear sympathetic. In truth, Jason's job didn't bother her. She didn't worry about him. She was positive he took care of himself when investigating crimes. Yes, it helped he'd been promoted to detective and no longer worked the beat shifts and routes. But even if he continued to hold that position, she trusted he took precautions along with the backup of the men that worked by his side.

Something in her expression must have given away her thoughts. The chief gave her a satisfied smile. "You can handle his job."

"I can."

"Good." He smacked his hand off the desk. "Now, tell me about yourself."

What the hell? Before she could filter, she popped out, "Why?"

Jason's boss didn't flinch, as if expecting her reaction. Or he was used to uncooperative women. "Something to hide?"

She couldn't tell if he was provoking or serious. He held a stoic demeanor, ideal for a chief of police, she assumed. Which made reading him a challenge.

She waved dismissively, afraid of raising the chief's internal warning. "No. There's nothing to tell really."

"Did you grow up around here?"

"No, I'm from upstate New York." She stuck to the mantra of always inserting a fraction of the truth. "I come from a rough upbringing. I moved here to start over and get away from that life."

Chief nodded. "It's hard to do. It can be discouraging. Less than a handful I can name off the top of my head managed to pull themselves out from their parents' lifestyle choices."

Hannah's vivid memory went back to that apartment building she grew up in. The loud noises of shouts, music, and sometimes gunfire along with stale scents of cigarettes, cooked drugs, and booze still haunted her. Her mother's overdosed moans, her father passed out on the sofa, almost lifeless, for days.

"Hannah." Chief's voice pulled her out of those wretched recollections. He didn't smile sympathetically. He didn't judge. He didn't look down on her pitifully. "You have my respect and admiration. I think of all the LEO wives we have, you'll be, by far, the most loyal and understanding. Welcome to the family."

Hannah's shame slammed into her. She lowered her head, her vision blurred with tears she desperately tried to blink back. She didn't deserve his respect. She didn't deserve to be accepted by these men. But she selfishly wanted it.

"Beautiful women shouldn't cry. You're not a pretty crier." Chief opened up a drawer behind his desk and tossed a box of tissues at her.

She caught the carton and snorted at his bluntness. "Never have been."

"At least you recognize you do have a fault."

"I have many, but I'm not giving you ammo."

He held up his hands. "I would never use your imperfections as weapons."

Yes he would, if only he knew.

Chief stood and gestured to the door. "Let me give you a tour."

She snatched a couple more tissues and followed. "Don't you have a wife to go home to?"

"No."

"Oh, are you single?"

"Do not even think about setting me up with one of your girlfriends." He held up a finger in warning.

"I don't have any girlfriends. Women tend to steer clear of me." They walked down a long hall, passing officers getting ready to head out on the late shift.

"I believe that. Most women would find you intimidating, I'm sure." He smirked and inspected her. "You really are a tiny thing, aren't you?"

"Small package. Big item."

He choked back a laugh. "And highly intelligent."

"Not really." Street smart, yeah.

"Don't insult yourself, Hannah. I do not take kindly to self-deprecation. Down this hall we have several rooms, including our break room, locker room, conference room, media room." They passed by open room after room, all of it very sterile and cold. Filing cabinets, tables, metal chairs, no windows to shine sunlight into the building. "Down there we have lockups and interrogation rooms."

An area she did not wish to visit.

They stopped outside a room when an officer approached the chief and handed him paperwork that required his signature. He introduced her as Campbell's future wife. While he pulled out a pen and signed away, her gaze wandered through the door of the room on her left. Her heart plummeted. A large white board centered the conference room. And close up photos of her in the middle of her heists hung from the board. Next to each picture, dates and times and places. That's when it smacked her upside the head.

She wasn't just playing with fire. She danced in the flames. Being with Jason had grounded her. Gave her normality. But those pictures, that board, put her world in perspective. She was wanted. By these men. And they actively hunted their fugitive.

Time to leave.

Hannah's breath escaped and her stomach cramped. A stabbing pain developed in her chest. She had to leave Jason. Leave the city. Leave Roy. She needed to do a complete upheaval and start over. Again.

A sudden need to vomit threatened to rise. Her world went dizzy. Leave Jason. How could she? How could she walk away from the man she loved? The only man to ever own her heart.

Hannah had to choose the right path. For too long she took the selfish route. Walking away now would save Jason from a worse heartbreak than destroying him in months or years down the road. Or when he had to arrest her, which scanning their work prominently displayed, she supposed should be considered imminent.

She took a deep breath, closed her eyes briefly, and turned to the chief. "I'm sorry, but I need to leave. I have a job interview in a half an hour and I want to be early."

Chief glanced down at her while he continued to go over the paperwork in front of him. He halted when their eyes met.

"Thank you for the tour. We'll have to finish another day." She scooted off before he could reply. At the end of the hallway, she spared a quick look over her shoulder. Jason's boss stared after her, his head slowly turning to his left where her unidentifiable pictures hung, and back to her. She watched awareness cross his handsome features.

"Hannah," he called after her.

She ignored him and hurried out to her car.

By the time the chief rushed outside to chase after her, she punched her car out of the parking lot of the police station. She figured she had almost no time to rush back to her apartment, snatch her pre-packed emergency duffle bag and suitcase, then hightail it out of the city. She wouldn't have time to leave Jason a note or say goodbye to Roy.

Tears streamed down her cheeks. She didn't want this. She never considered their end playing out this way. She wanted Jason, a home, a family and friends. She wanted mundane. Hannah bitterly swiped at her tears. She had no one to blame but herself. Her stupid decision to come to the police station was on her. The path she chose to pull herself out of her parents' mess and unnecessarily continue was of her own making. But it still rankled, knowing that years ago, she had no other recourse.

Ten minutes later, Hannah pulled into her assigned parking spot. She caught the elevator alone for the short ride to the sixth floor. When she stepped off the elevator, she stopped. Her heart plummeted to the ground floor. Fear washed over her.

They found her.

The men who her parents consistently owed money lounged in the hallway, seven men lying in wait. Guy number one spotted her, an evil sneer crossing his haggard features.

Every lesson of the self-defense classes she took kicked in. She pressed the button on her keychain, engaging the apartment cameras, hoping Roy would call the police for help. She didn't have time to speculate the pros and cons between choosing law enforcement or the mob.

Hannah spun to run toward the stairs. The elevator doors would never close in time for a quick escape.

She didn't reach the stairwell. Hands grabbed her from behind, clamping over her mouth and pinning her arms to the side. She kicked back, connecting with a shin, following up with a swing back and hitting a groin. She fell to the floor in a heap.

Hannah scrambled to the exit door while pulling herself up. She pushed on the steel bar–

\*\*\*

"Wakey, wakey sunshine," a baritone voice cajoled.

Hannah's eyes blinked open. A throbbing pain in her skull pulsed behind her eyes. She moaned. As she grew more alert, she took stock in her body. Both arms securely held outstretched to each side, like they'd yank her limbs from her body when given the go ahead.

Her head bobbled as she tried to lift the heavy weight.

"There she is." She recognized the man as the one who'd broken her legs in the past. He toyed with a lock of her hair. "I like the red. Much nicer than the light dirty brown. We almost didn't recognize you. You're scrawny."

She tried to scan her surroundings but her vision bounced. Her eyes literally hurt. What the hell did they do to her?

A hand took her by the chin, squeezed, and lifted her head. "Your parents owe my boss a lot of money. Do you have two hundred grand laying around this expensive apartment?"

"Two hundred?" she croaked, shocked at the obscene amount.

"Yes, sweetheart." He squeezed her jaw tighter. A vice clamping down on her face. She wanted to cry out in pain, but used every ounce of will power to keep her misery inside. She couldn't show weakness.

"I don't have it."

"Really?" He made a show of casing her pricey belongings. "That's too bad." He held out his palm to the side. Someone handed him a lead pipe. Total loan shark cheesy intimidation, but effective.

Before he swung at her, she blurted out, trying to reason with the unreasonable. "I'll get you the money."

"Oh, I know you will, honey. You'll get me every last dime. You see, your parents didn't just take our product and not pay. They literally came into the boss's home and stole. They stole his televisions, his kids' gaming systems, his wife's gold jewelry, his Rolex and whatever else worth of value they could get their grubby hands onto. Do you know what they did afterward?"

No. She really didn't want to know.

"They hauled it all into his Escalade and Porsche and stole the cars. By the time we found those cars, they had trashed everything. Sold what they could and crossed over the Canadian border. So guess who gets to buy dear ol' Mommy and Daddy out of trouble?" He drew the pipe back over his shoulder.

"I can't get you the money with broken legs," she spat out before he swung forward.

He lowered the metal. "True."

She took advantage of the unguarded moment, kicked up her right leg and connected with a knee cap, the man holding her right side collapsing to the ground in writhing pain. A spin kick and she connected to the thigh of the guy on the left, a crack reverberated throughout the apartment. Another man charged and she punched up with the heel of her hand, connected with his nose, breaking it. Blood spewed out, hitting her in the face.

A blow to the back of head from behind knocked her to the ground. She caught herself on all fours. Her vision went hazy as pain ripped through her head. She desperately fought her body wanting to black out. She took a kick to the stomach, a severe pain knocking the wind out of her. Hannah collapsed to the floor, holding her belly, audibly gasping to get air into her lungs. She tried to crawl away from the man who towered her, furious as hell.

"You bitch. You just created more carnage that I can handle." He pulled her hair, human empathy void in those black eyes. "You will get me that money or you'll end up in a shallow grave, somewhere no one will ever find you, but not before I give you to my boss and his men to have some fun."

She tried to sweep his legs out from underneath him but someone clamped her limbs to the cold floor.

"Give her something to remember but don't beat her enough where she can't get us our money," the man snarled.

Hannah lost track of how many men took a turn punching her in the face, stomach, and lower back. For all she knew, one man did the damage. White and black spots inhibited her vision. Her leg and arm muscles cramped with each blow. She held her breath, anticipating the next punch or kick.

"Enough." The man knelt in front of her as she laid on her living room floor, a shooting pain ripping through her rib cage. Her face went numb. A metallic taste filled her mouth.

He took her chin into his hands and tilted her face upward. "You have one month."

She spit the blood that pooled in her mouth into his face.

He smirked. "Not the first time a woman has done such a thing. You're lucky I want the boss's money more than I want you dead."

Hannah watched him stand and three men help the injured out of her apartment. She attempted to crawl toward the contents of her purse that had been dumped across the room, near the kitchen. She needed her phone to call Roy to get her a cab to the hospital. She needed medical attention. Again. Fucking bastards.

Hannah gave up and collapsed. A few minutes of rest would give her enough energy to make another effort to get her phone.

## 28

"I can't believe you spent that amount of money on a rock." Dean took a swig of his beer, while his focus followed the path of a cute brunette that pranced past them.

"She's worth every dime." The black velvet box sat perfectly safe inside his jacket pocket. He was not about to let the expensive piece of jewelry out of his care until he slipped it onto Hannah's delicate finger.

His phone buzzed. He pulled it out and glowered at the caller ID. He didn't recognize the number, so stuck the device back into his pocket. Let it go to voicemail.

"Do you have a date set?" Tyler asked.

Of all his brothers, Tyler seemed the most at odds with the announcement. He seemed curious, yet offended and jealous concurrently. Jason didn't understand his issue.

"No. I only asked her last week. I'm more concerned with getting her into my house first."

Nick's uncanny observant skills didn't disappoint. "You're afraid she'll bolt."

"Honestly, yes."

"Then why the fuck did you ask her?" Dean gaped.

"I love her. I'll do everything in my power to make certain she knows I'm her home. That no matter where she goes, she won't be happy unless I'm with her." He took a long drag of his beer. He truly meant his proclamation. He recognized enough that Hannah's personality and history made her ripe for taking off on him. But he also saw that she craved love. The interaction with his parents proved she wanted a normal family unit. He could provide that for her. If she didn't get into her own head. He just needed to break down those demons that existed and every once in a while reared their ugly head, when she let her guard down. Really, if he showered her with affection, it should be easy enough.

Funny how one woman could make him change his entire outlook. How she could make him distinguish the life he lived before her was nothing more than a shadow of itself. Nonexistent. Lonely. Unfulfilled. Hannah changed his world and he refused to go back to his old life, embracing bachelorhood.

His phone buzzed again. He pulled it out of his pocket. That same unknown number.

"Is that her calling to check up on you?" Dean asked, insulted.

"No. Don't know this number."

"Answer it," Tyler said. "You should never leave a call go to voicemail. Unless it's an ex you're avoiding."

All three men stared at him.

"What?" Tyler asked.

"Dude, you do not do that to Kayla?" Nick said.

Tyler had the sense to blush. "Sometimes."

"Idiot. Man up and answer the damn phone." Dean smacked his beer out of his hand, the bottle landing on the floor with a clatter.

Jason answered his. "Hello?"

"Is this Jason Campbell?"

"Who is this?"

His brothers grew quiet, their attention now focused in on his call. Their natural instincts on display as Dean automatically checked for his weapon at his side.

"You need to get to Hannah's apartment, now," the unknown male voice said. "She's in trouble."

"Who is this?"

"It doesn't matter. You need to get there immediately. And make sure you bring backup." The line disconnected.

Jason turned and flew out of the bar. He was vaguely aware of his brothers on his heels.

"Jason," Dean yelled.

"I have to get to Hannah's."

"What's wrong?" Nick demanded.

Jason jumped into his car, his partner and brothers diving in with him. "I don't know. The man said get to Hannah's, she's in trouble."

"Jason, this could be trap," Dean said.

Nick and Tyler's phones started to ring. Dean's went off as well. All three answered and muttered into their phones. Jason ignored their conversations, concentrating on weaving in and out of traffic. When Dean hung up, he turned to Jason. "That was Chief. He needs to talk to you. I told him what was happening. He's sending a unit to Hannah's apartment."

Eight minutes later, they managed to beat their backup to Hannah's apartment. All four rushed up to the sixth floor through the stairwell. Before they opened the door, Nick spun on Jason, bracing a hand against his chest. "I take lead on this. Tyler backs me up. Dean and you bring in the rear. We don't know what this is, we need to be careful. You received a random call about your fiancée. This has set up written all over it."

Jason wanted to disagree. He wanted to scream and burst through the door. But his ingrained law enforcement mentality took over, agreeing with Nick's level head. He nodded, unable to form words yet. His mind scrambled. What the hell was going on?

Nick opened the heavy steel door slowly, his gun drawn. When Nick was certain the hall was clear, he led out, Tyler flanking him. Dean and Jason covered their backs to make certain they didn't get ambushed. Jason's blood pumped, his mind going blank as every bit of training he ever received kicked in. He heard a loud television from one of the apartments, the elevator running a few floors below, the humming from the florescent lights. He heard Dean's footsteps beside him, his own breathing through his nose.

They rounded the corner, the hallway empty. That didn't put them in the clear. Someone could be taking cover behind a closed apartment door and assault them, shooting up the enclosed space.

Nick approached Hannah's door, standing off to the right. Tyler positioned to the left, Dean and Jason behind him. Nick pounded on the door. They waited. An eternity.

Nick pounded again. "Hannah?"

Nothing.

Jason grew antsy. "See if the door is unlocked."

Nick glared his direction. He turned the knob slowly. The door clicked, releasing from its closed position. Tyler reached up and pushed it open.

"Hannah?" Nick called again. "It's Detective Nick Butler. Are you home?"

Nick glanced down and back up to Tyler. Tyler followed his direction, his face twisting into a frown. Both men lifted their weapons into an aimed stance.

"What is it?" Jason demanded.

"Blood," Tyler answered.

Nick glared his partner's direction.

Jason went to storm the apartment but Dean hauled him back. "Let us go in."

Nick went in first, carefully sticking close to the wall. Tyler followed. Dean and Jason trailing, their eyes on their brother's backs.

"Holy fuck," Nick said.

Jason couldn't take any more. He left his position and pushed past his brothers.

Laying in a heap on the floor near the kitchen was Hannah's broken, lifeless body. Jason rushed to her side.

"Hannah?" He pushed her wet, matted hair off her face.

Her eyes fluttered open. "Jason?"

Dean was at her other side, taking her pulse. "It's weak."

"Tyler's calling for ambulance." Nick came in from doing a sweep of the apartment.

"No," Hannah feebly protested. "Just take me to the hospital. No ambulance."

Carefully they rolled her onto her back. She groaned out in extreme pain with the movement.

Tyler had the EMT background. He checked her breathing and swiftly scanned her body for wounds.

"Hannah, baby," Jason said, his voice cracking.

Her body went stiff as a board, as if afraid to move. Jason's heart broke. He wanted his spitfire of a girl to sit up and be pissed off over her condition. He'd take care of her, but that minimal show of strength would give him profound relief. Jason took her left hand into his.

"Who did this to you?" Tyler asked. At least he had the wherewithal to perform his detective, law abiding duties.

"Hannah, I'm here." He leaned down and kissed her swollen lips. Her eyes began to swell, as well as a deep bruise forming on her right cheek. An open cut above her left eye had blood dripping onto the pristine floor. Jason grabbed a tissue off an end table and held it to the wound to stop the bleeding.

"Hannah, you have to tell us what happened to you besides the injuries we can see." Dean knelt next to Jason.

"Who did this to you?" Nick asked.

"Just get me to the hospital." She tried to sit up on her own, but barely budged.

"Stop it," Jason growled. "Cooperate for once."

Suddenly a flurry of activity surrounded them, including Chief. "Jason, let the EMTs do their job."

Jason refused to release her hand.

Hannah groaned again. "No fucking ambulance."

"You don't have a say in this, Hannah," Jason bit out, becoming frustrated with her lack of compliance to take care of her.

"He can't work this, boss," Dean said.

"No, he can't. You three take this. Let him go with her," Chief said.

Jason stayed with Hannah as the EMTs worked on her, placed her on a gurney, and wheeled her down to the ambulance. Who the hell beat the fuck out of his girl? Who dared to enter the security of her home and assault her? Fury combined with fear flooded him.

He stayed by her side, stroking her hand and arm, whispering to her. Assuring her he refused to leave her side. The entire time she gripped his palm, as if holding onto him for strength and support. He prayed her injuries weren't life threatening. He prayed for her quick recovery. God, he couldn't take the sight of her incapacitated. This shot straight to his heart. He wanted to bear this pain for her.

But he remembered that day they first met. When Hannah knocked his shopping cart to the ground. His Hannah fought. She fought to survive her parents' shitty upbringing. She fought to make a life for herself. She wouldn't allow someone to walk into her apartment and take liberties on her without taking them on blow for blow. Which left the question, how much damage to her body had been done that didn't show from the outside. A tear slipped down his cheek. If he'd only gone home after he bought the ring, this would not have happened. If he hadn't gone for the ring and waited to take her with him to choose a design she loved, he would have been home to protect her. If Jason hadn't listened to her and gone to happy hour for a couple of fucking beers, they would have been at his home, nowhere near her apartment for this assault.

Jason would never forgive himself for leaving his Hannah unprotected.

## 29

The annoying beep from the heart monitor stabbed at Hannah's sore, heavy head. An agonizing moan gurgled from her throat.

"Hannah." The distraught yet sexy, familiar voice tugged at her. "Hannah, baby, how are you? Do you need me to get the nurse?"

Her head lolled to her right, where Jason sat by her side in the examination room of the hospital. She'd been there for hours getting x-rays and tests and being poked and prodded. She tried to take a deep breath but winced at the pain under her right breast. The fuckers. How did they expect her to get them their money with a damn broken rib? Idiots. Luckily no other damage had been done. Bastards.

"Don't breathe in deep."

"Really?" She was unable to control her sarcasm.

Jason frowned.

"Sorry." She didn't need to take her annoyance and ire on him.

Jason perched himself on the edge of her bed. "Who did this to you?"

Hannah couldn't reveal the information he desperately wanted to know. No matter how badly she wanted to. Or how she ached to confess her troubles, hoping Jason would help with the burden. Too much would lead back to her crimes. Her freedom would be in jeopardy. Jason's love for her would vanish. He'd be forced to choose between his job or her and she'd lose. She couldn't do that to him, or herself.

"I don't know," she lied.

He hesitated, his intense gaze analyzing her. She understood his personality well enough to know he battled within to grill her.

"All right." He clasped her hand and kissed the back of it. He lovingly brushed her hair off her sweaty face, leaned down and kissed her. Even that hurt. "You might not remember the details this second but we'll discuss it later. Once you've been discharged. I'll get some cold compresses for your eye, cheek, and mouth. You rest while we wait for the doctor to choose whether or not to keep you overnight."

Insurmountable regret annihilated her. She was grateful he dropped the questioning. Realistically, she knew she'd have to provide answers soon enough. But her depleted body wanted to succumb to sleep. "Thank you."

"You're welcome, baby."

Her lids grew heavy as soon as Jason left the room. She could relax knowing he stationed himself nearby and wouldn't leave her side. As long as he remained within close proximity, he'd temporarily keep his boss and his partners from drilling her.

*** 

When Hannah's eyes flickered open again, the small, curtained off exam area resembled a hospital staff party thrown in her honor. She found Jason next to her bed, papers in hand.

"Jason," she wheezed.

Tossing the stack aside, he jumped from his chair and took her hand. He smiled, his handsome features a relieving and welcoming sight.

"Hi." His voice cracked, the emotion taking a toll on him.

"Hi."

"You ready to go home soon? They're arguing over whether to admit you. But there's not enough beds. Doc says you should be fine." He stroked her cheek, the sensation foreign against her numb face.

"Yes."

Jason straightened upright. "Is someone going to tell us about discharging Miss Lakely? Or do I have to start getting irate? She wants to go home."

A nurse came in to take her vitals. "How are you feeling?"

"Like I've had the shit beat out of me."

"Yes, I can imagine." The nurse smiled kindly. "Let them hash out your status while I get your temperature and blood pressure."

"My pressure will probably read high, it always has, even as a teen." A consequence of the abhorrent amount of stress placed upon her.

"Good to know. Pain will also contribute to a higher registered reading, especially under your condition," the nurse said. "You may get lightheaded and dizzy, that could be a side effect from the pain meds as well."

She hated taking any form of pain medication. She feared she might fall into her parents' habits, inheriting their addiction. As soon as Hannah settled wherever she would place her head to recuperate, she would trash the meds and heal on her own. She prayed whatever they gave her in the IV didn't take hold and she'd end up repeating patterns.

"Thanks." She was testy and anxious and already tired of the noise in the room.

The nurse busied herself, taking Hannah's vitals. When she finally left the room, Jason stepped up to the side of the bed, his features ripe with concern.

"It's going to be another hour. He's keeping you here under observation for a bit." Jason stroked her arm. He noticeably wanted to care for her but had no clue how to go about accomplishing the task.

Tears slid down the sides of her face. She just wanted to get into her own bed and cry herself to sleep and forget about the dire circumstances of her life. Was that too much to ask?

"Who did this to you? You have to tell me." Jason's pleading and her mental and physical exhaustion almost evoked a confession of everything. It was on the tip of her tongue. She opened her mouth and closed it. Twice.

He didn't give her a chance to admit her failings. "You fought, didn't you? My girl would never go down without a fight."

Jason visibly grappled a barrage of emotions, pride and fear being at the forefront.

"Who did this Hannah?" he whispered. "Was it the men who've come after you before?"

Life changing decisions. Either tell the truth or lie, and hope Jason refused to push. Neither choice had any pros. No matter which path she picked, there would be severe consequences. It now depended on how involved she wanted Jason. How much she allowed herself to open up to him. Jason and his partner and friends would never find the men. The loan sharks didn't want to be found. But Jason would break his back trying to put her assailants behind bars. If she told him the truth, it would expeditiously lead back to her jewelry store thievery. Those ramifications would be far more reaching than anything the loan sharks did to her.

She promptly decided before she changed her mind. "I don't know who they were. They weren't from my parents' indiscretions. They wanted my purse and wanted anything they could take from my apartment. I saw them hanging around in the hallway but didn't pay attention. I thought there was a party or something at one of the neighbors. When I opened the door, I got shoved in from behind. I did fight. As much as I could."

Jason's face fell. He knew she was lying.

"Nothing was taken from the apartment, honey." He paused, as if weighing his words carefully. "You don't have to protect whoever did this to you. I'll make certain you're safe. You're not alone any longer. How many people were there? Was it one, more than one? Please help me find whoever had the audacity to lay a finger on you so I can put them away and you can sleep peacefully at night."

She'd love to be able to revel in a tranquil rest for one night. Without jerking awake or screaming herself out of a deep slumber. She desperately wanted to tell him. She wanted to release all her stress and dump this problem onto Jason's lap. She knew he'd take over and do everything in his power to shield her from harm. But he couldn't. If she involved the police, eventually the man her parents stole from would catch her, and when he did, she'd disappear, never to be heard or seen from again. Her body would never be found. She'd die a slow and agonizing death. And Jason would spend the rest of his life wondering what happened to her. He might move on, but he would never move past her disappearance. Hannah's lie was the best path for both of them.

"I don't know, Jason." A piece of her soul died with each blatant lie. "I wish I did, but I don't."

"Could you give descriptions if I brought in a sketch artist?" He grappled for anything.

She had to give him a small bone. "I'll do my best."

He smiled slightly. "Good."

"How did you find me?"

Jason propped himself on the edge of the bed and took both her hands. "I got a phone call. Very cryptic. That I needed to get to your place. The guys had to keep me in line, afraid it was a trap. We tried to trace the call but it was scrambled."

Fucking Roy. Thank goodness he turned on the camera feed when she'd hit the remote, but instead of calling 911, he contacted Jason.

Hannah had given him Jason's phone number weeks ago, just in case of an emergency. Jason didn't know. In fact, he hadn't met Roy and she kept any conversation about her best friend to a minimum. That may be her one saving grace at this moment.

"It must have been one of the neighbors." She tried to plant a seed.

Jason shook his head. "We interviewed all of them."

"Someone could be lying."

"Could, but doubtful. Most of your neighbors were troubled over the incident that happened while they were home but didn't hear any struggle or notice any non-residents lingering about. Only one resident on the floor wasn't home." Jason toyed with her left ring finger. He reached into his jacket pocket, pulled out a black velvet box and slowly opened it.

Hannah gasped. A three carat diamond sparkled at her. It was the most beautiful piece of jewelry she'd laid eyes upon. A flawless round, halo setting in 14k white gold. How could Jason afford such an expensive ring on his salary? Her heart crushed under the knowledge Jason bought her a ring he assuredly took the time to personally choose based on the love he had for her. His choice perfect for her personality. Exactly what she would have picked for herself. She didn't deserve the priceless ring. Tears spilled over.

"This is where I was this evening. Instead of with you. I'll never forgive myself for not being with you to prevent the attack." He slid the ring onto her finger, lifted her hand, and kissed the ring.

"It wasn't your fault. I would never blame you for not being there."

"I know, because you won't allow me to carry some of your burden."

She cringed at his truthful observation. "I'm trying."

Jason didn't respond, his sullen stare searched her, like answers would suddenly come from her if he willed them to. He cleared his throat. Her heart ached, physically pained in her chest cavity, at his deep love for her and her betrayal of his heart.

"Don't do that to me again," Jason whispered, leaned down and reverently kissed her lips.

Hannah refused to comment further. Unfortunately her next necessary step would break both of them. As soon as Jason gave her a moment alone, she would make one phone call and slip out of the hospital, leaving the love of her life behind. For his sake.

## 30

Jason didn't understand why Hannah lied to him. A normal person would have suffered traumatically under the conditions she survived. An assault wasn't something anyone could shake off. But his Hannah fought tooth and nail, no matter the circumstances. She possessed a different type of mentality. One that he witnessed a handful of times as an officer and detective. She survived. Anyway she could, she pulled a deep strength to the surface and fought internally and externally. But now that he entered the picture, Hannah could lean on him. Jason constantly reminded her that they were a team. So why did she lie? Was it old habits die hard? Was it that she didn't trust him?

Instead of digging further, his detective skills threatening to blow up into full mode, he decided to let it be. For now.

Jason leaned down and kissed the ring he placed on her finger, again. It fit her a bit snug, but only due to the swelling. "I love you."

"I love you." She choked on a sob.

"Rest. I'm going to the waiting room and let everyone know we're waiting for your discharge papers."

Her brows slid together. "Who's here?"

"My parents, my brothers, Chief." He smiled slightly at the fact his family and extended family showed concern over his girl. Three in the morning and they all hadn't slept. Fellow officers stopped by, those on duty bringing food and drinks.

Hannah's bruised eyes watered. "They're all here?"

Jason nodded and kissed her forehead. "They are. They love you as much as I do."

Her body trembled and she cried out in pain. "My ribs."

"Baby, stay calm. It's going to take a few weeks for those to heal. I'm moving your stuff into my house—"

Hannah went to protest, but in a timely entrance, the nurse came into the room before his girl could spout some nonsense he'd disagree with.

"Okay, honey, time for your pain meds. You need them to allow your body to relax and heal." She held out tiny paper cup with one pill and another with some water.

"I don't want to take that. Can I have some ibuprofen instead?" Her voice shook, small and unsure.

"Jason," she stammered, silently beseeching him to understand and explain why she refused to take any form of drug.

Hannah squeezed his hand tightly. As expected, she wouldn't want narcotics. "She has a family history of addiction."

The nurse smiled warmly. "We can try it but if it doesn't work I'll have the doctor prescribe a low dose."

She visibly relaxed and breathed out a sigh of relief, cringing at the slight movement.

"I'll be back shortly." The nurse swiftly left the room and he followed.

Hannah focused on Jason. "I love you."

Her inflection stopped him on his way out of the room. Why had she professed her love in that manner? Almost like a finality.

"I love you, too."

Those beautiful blue eyes took on a sadness he'd never seen from her before. Jason hesitated, about to inquire further but elected to shake it off. He couldn't hound her. It took a lot of self-restraint to hold down his inner cop mode and not annoyingly interrogate her. She needed rest. More than likely his inner turmoil over Hannah's condition and lack of cooperation impelled him to hear a tone that didn't exist.

\*\*\*

Jason stepped into the waiting area and his mother jumped up from her seat and rushed him. "Is Hannah all right?"

"She is, Mom. She'll be fine. Do you mind sitting with her for a while. I'm going to her apartment to get clothes she'll need. I'm bringing her home with me to help her recover." He wrapped an arm around his mom's slender shoulders.

"Absolutely, sweetheart." She patted his hand and pushed up on her tiptoes to kiss his cheek. "You take care of her. She needs you."

"I will."

His mother scooted off toward the large doors that led to the exam rooms.

His father followed, shaking his head and grinning indulgently. "You've given your mother the best gift a son ever could. A future daughter-in-law. Your mom's on cloud nine."

His dad laid a supportive hand on his shoulder as he passed.

Dean approached, his weary features in need of a shave. "How is she?"

"Groggy. In some pain. But she refuses meds. She's tough." He rubbed at his tired eyes. His muscles ached. His body exhausted from worry. His mind numb from stifling distress over who hurt his girl.

"Did you ask her any questions?" Nick handed him a hot cup of coffee.

"Thanks. I did." He took a sip, the liquid luke warm and tart.

"She said she doesn't know who the attackers were. She did try to fend them off. Said they were there to rob her." Jason recited Hannah's entire vague recollection.

"Odd," Tyler said.

"What?" Jason asked.

"Did she say how many there were?" Tyler asked.

Jason gritted his teeth. "No. What's your problem?"

Yes, some things with Hannah's recollection didn't add up. But she'd been through a vicious attack. Lapses could and should be expected. They would continue to quiz her until they got what they needed, putting the pieces together. That was their job.

"I think she knew them," Tyler bluntly said.

"What the fuck?" Jason reared back.

Dean stepped between him and the rookie detective, a firm hand placed center on his chest. "Listen, we know you're personally involved here. We get it. And we're just as upset as you are that someone came into Hannah's place and had the gall to lay a hand on her. All we want is to catch whoever hurt her and put them in cuffs. That's it. Tyler's theory is that she knew her attacker and thinks there's more than one. I don't have a theory yet. There are too many holes."

"Same here," Nick said.

Dean flipped a thumb Tyler's way. "That's from experience. Youngblood over here has watched too much television and movies."

Tyler crossed his arms over his chest and stuck out his chin. "No I haven't. I'm just basing off what we do know."

"And what do we know?" Jason challenged.

Luckily the waiting area emptied except for his brothers. Chief stood off to the side, oddly quiet, allowing the scene to play out.

Tyler went to respond but stopped. He had no evidence to back up his assumptions. They didn't know anything until the evidence they found and pieced together along with Hannah's statement completed the puzzle. They had no fingerprints except for his and hers. They had no witnesses. They had nothing. Why the newer building didn't have security cameras, Jason didn't know. Totally unheard of in today's day and age. Tyler jumping to premature conclusions without firm evidence pissed him off.

"You be very careful, O'Neill." Jason pegged him, his temper spiking. "She's going to be my wife."

Tyler backed away, his hands up. "I'm only speculating."

"Well don't." He launched his cup into the garbage. "We follow evidence. Speculating is for amateurs."

Jason stormed out of the waiting room, slamming through the door, the metal handles whacking the wall.

Dean rushed after him. "Buddy, where are you going?"

"I have to go to Hannah's and pack items for her to stay with me."

"I'll come with you." Dean pulled out his keys. "Let me drive."

Jason abruptly stopped and wheeled on his friend. "Do you agree with Tyler?"

"I told you I don't have a theory." Dean opened his car door.

"That's not what I asked." Jason slapped the roof of Dean's car.

Dean leaned on the hood of his sedan. "We have no idea what happened, partner. How could we? You haven't allowed us near her. We believe jewelry might be missing, but we haven't interviewed her yet. Tyler's premature in stating his thoughts on the case. Our only witness hasn't been questioned. Until we are able to, all we can do is wait and go over what evidence we do have. But I'm sure she'll be cooperative."

"She agreed to talk to a sketch artist."

"Fantastic." Dean gave him an encouraging smile. "We'll find out what happened. We can send the artist in the morning and back again in a couple days. See if she remembers anything else a few days later."

Jason didn't want to admit he had some reservations about the vibe from Hannah's obvious lie. He refused to say a word until he figured out why she withheld the truth. After all, there had to be a valid reason, right? Hannah wouldn't lie to him without what she perceived an extreme motive. After a few days, she would realize she needed to open up to him. Jason would subtly work on fixing that awful trait.

*** 

Jason placed a pile of Hannah's clothing on the living room sofa. While he had gone through her toiletries, Dean roamed the apartment. His partner didn't say a word or touch one object. Instead, he carefully eyed the surroundings, scribbling in a small notepad. Dean may play the nonchalant, carefree guy, but most people weren't aware that they only saw a front. An act. He was a damn good detective. Those closest to the man understood why the playboy veil developed five years ago, when his life fractured after the loss of his unborn son.

Jason returned to Hannah's bedroom and opened her closet door. After rummaging through the clothes rack, he knelt down on the floor to choose a couple pairs of the plethora of shoes laid out before him. He picked a few runners and flats and as he placed the ones he wouldn't take back in their appropriate spots, he eyed a stuffed black duffle bag shoved in the back of the closet. Curious, Jason pulled it out and opened it. As soon as he saw the contents, his heart dropped.

A getaway bag. Clothes, money, a passport, everything she would need for a quick escape. Putting two and two together, Hannah knew her attackers. And odds the individuals led back to her parents were great. That would be the only logical reason for this bag.

Jason sat back on his heels, his chest feeling like it could collapse on him. His girl couldn't confide in him over her fear. And worse, that she prepared to leave him at any given moment. Probably without warning or contact. His blood went from cold to hot. How could she think it was all right to consider such a horrendous plan? How could she not understand he'd worry like hell and move heaven and earth to find her? How the hell could the woman he'd been sleeping with and professed his love to think that abandoning him instead of turning to him was acceptable?

He needed answers immediately. He would fucking get them. One way or another.

Jason loved Hannah. He'd do anything for her. Protect her any way he could. But he would not tolerate her callously disappearing on him like his heart or love didn't matter.

Jason lurched to his feet and stalked out the apartment, Dean once again on his heels. Hannah had questions to answer. Despite her condition, he refused to shelve his inquiries. She owed him an explanation.

## 31

Hannah's heavy body stirred out of a deep sleep.

"Hannah." A stern voice ordered to rise her.

She tried to blink open the heavy weights of her closed lids.

"Hannah, you need to wake." Jason's voice was curt and cold. Not his usual easy-going tone he saved for her.

She managed to pry open her eyelids, but her head didn't want to turn his direction. He appeared in front of her. His haggard features, mouth turned down and pursed lips didn't bode well.

"Is something wrong with me?" She was afraid of what happened while she'd conked out. How long had she been asleep? She slid a glance to the wall clock. An hour. When would they finally discharge her?

"You're fine. All tests came back normal," he answered and pulled up a stool. "But you have bigger issues than that."

"What?" She breathed and struggled to rise. What did he discover?

"Stay down. You aren't in any condition to sit up." Deep lines around his eyes suggested his tiredness finally set in.

"I'm fine. What's wrong?" She didn't like his snippy tone.

"If you have to take off, for whatever reason, do you plan on contacting me or just leaving as if our relationship never existed?" His face was a blank mask.

What the hell was he talking about? "Jason, I don't understand."

"I found your getaway bag, Hannah."

She dizzied. Her world actually spun. She closed her eyes to get her bearings. Did he find the other bag? The one that contained the money she got paid for the diamonds? Or the small satchel inside the bag that held leftover diamonds she'd stolen and had designed into a bracelet to sell if needed?

"Don't you fucking close your eyes on me. I deserve an answer."

Her eyes popped open, her vision blurred from hot tears. She never wanted to face this moment. Jason's questions would become more involved. Finding that duffle, he probably already pieced together that her attackers originated from her parents. It wouldn't take much to piece together. Her fiancé wasn't a stupid man. Yet she'd treated him like one. She toyed with him despite the fact he didn't deserve such treatment. She played with his heart because he made her fully aware of something she never had. Love. Jason loved her, yet she'd been greedy and self-destructive.

"No." Might as well rip off the band-aid. Deep down, he had to already know the answer.

His sharp inhale echoed throughout the room.

"No?" he breathed. "You were just going to get up and leave me?"

The wretched pain that hung onto his question burned into her soul. She'd never be able to take back that horribly truthful answer.

"They were men who dealt with your parents, weren't they? Tell me the truth. I already know."

No matter how crushing it would be to both of them, the time had come to end this. "Jason, I love you. I've never loved anyone in my life. You are my first and only true love. But this isn't going to work out between us. We need to go our separate ways."

"Wait, what?" he yelped. "What the hell, Hannah? All you have to do is answer my questions. We'll hunt for the men who did this to you and everything will be fine. Why would you end our relationship? I asked justifiable questions? That makes no sense."

"You'll never find the men who did this to me. I'm not going to give you any information. I can't. They'll come back and your life will be in danger and I won't risk that." She sat up and swung her legs over the side of the bed. Time to get the hell out of Dodge and try to pick up the pieces of her shattered heart.

"You don't need to worry about me. I'm a cop, Hannah. I take care of myself and my family." He stood suddenly, the stool shooting across the room and hitting the back wall. Jason paced beside her bed, raking his hand down his face.

He was so beautiful for a man. From the way that he moved—a smooth, graceful glide—to the way he held himself—confident but not cocky. Every single thing about him called to her. Drew her into him. Even now, when she needed to hold firm, she wanted to retract her words and allow him to takeover. But she'd couldn't cave. She'd come too far in her survival to toss a wrench into her life. Not falling for Jason in the first place may have prevented all this.

"Jason," she slipped her feet into a pair of ballet flats, "we won't work out. I will have to leave eventually. It's best to end this now."

He came to her side and knelt down, his face reddened. He took her hands into his. "No, this doesn't have to end now. You're frightened. I get that. All you have to do is allow me to help you. It can be out of your hands now. I'll tell the team and we'll search for these men. There's no reason for you to run. It's too dangerous for you to be alone. You stay here, allow me to protect you, we put the bad guys in jail. There. Done."

And she'd end up dead.

"Jason," she whispered.

"Yes, baby?"

"We're through."

\*\*\*

Hannah glanced down at her phone, hoping a message came through overnight, waiting for her. Nothing. She sank further into the sofa in Roy's living room, the early morning sun peeking through the drawn shades. A complete contrast to her misery. She needed to get up to go for her routine jog. But her mind and body didn't jump at the task. After she broke Jason's heart a couple weeks ago, he left the hospital and didn't return. His partner Dean showed up, treating her like she was the worst woman who ever existed. She couldn't call his tone nasty, it held more of a curtness, when he spoke to her. They rushed a sketch artist in before she left the hospital. That man didn't exactly exude kindness, either. More than likely, he knew she lied the entire time she falsely described her assailants.

Hannah pulled herself upright and stretched as much as her ribcage allowed. Two weeks after she'd been beaten, she finally started to feel somewhat normal. She could perform a light cardio routine despite her rib condition. Weights and kickboxing and self-defense classes continued to be on hold. Every once in a while, when she moved a certain way, a pain jabbed through her chest. A cracked rib or a broken heart, she couldn't decipher between the two.

She trudged to Roy's tiny bathroom and changed into her workout attire. What time he went to bed last night, she didn't know. He'd been working relentlessly on developing a plan for McIntyre's, now that Hannah's hand was forced to come up with money quickly. Despite his objections, he couldn't argue that the store held the most bang for the buck needed. Now he concentrated on making certain she could get in and out without incident.

Hannah shoved her feet into her running shoes, grabbed her phone, and left the apartment. Once outside, she started off walking a brisk pace. The mornings grew colder, the fall season settling in. She favored this time of year. She loved jeans and long sleeved T-shirts. She admired the changing of the leaves, seeing symbolism in the different colors and comparing it to her own life. She may lose her leaves every now and again, but the roots remained no matter where the wind took her. She'd used that comparison toward her parents for as long as she could remember. But contemplating it in a different perspective, since meeting and falling in love with

Jason, she realized her roots were the ones she planted herself. Her own morality and decision making not instilled by her parents. Hannah chose her path. Oh, it was too easy to blame her parents, but essentially she had choices in every personal decision in her life. Whether or not they were the correct ones, well, only outcomes determined that.

Hannah started a light jog, her ribs slightly protesting, but she worked through the injury. She needed to get back into shape as soon as possible. Once she finished with McIntyre's, she planned to move from Pittsburgh and this time take Roy with her. She finally got him to agree, after assuring him she'd make the move as minimally stressful as possible.

"We'll go someplace warm," she'd said.

"I don't think I can do it." Roy nervously bounced his legs while seated in his computer chair, clicking through the photos of an apartment Hannah found in Florida.

"I'll take care of you. We'll do it like last time. I'll move everything out of the apartment first. You'll be last." She sat next to him, taking his hands into hers and squeezing.

"I don't want you to leave me alone." Roy's worry and need to stay with his only friend trumped his fear of the outside world. Hannah couldn't have been more grateful to have him.

"Never."

When she snuck out of the hospital after receiving her discharge papers, she went back to her apartment, picked up some of the clothes she found in a pile on the living room floor, and went straight to

Roy's. Her best friend took her in and nursed her back to health. She would never be able to repay the undeserving hospitality he's shown her over the years. Which, as always, brought her back to thoughts of Jason. She crossed a main intersection that led to a local park.

For three days after Hannah had been discharged, Jason tried contacting her, but she didn't answer her phone. It comforted her knowing he refused to let go. But the calls stopped on day four. Just over two weeks later and Hannah's heart was destroyed with the realization Jason moved on. She glanced down at her left hand, the diamond still in place. She couldn't part with it. She didn't want to part with it. The right thing to do would be to send it to Jason. But when was the last time she did the right thing?

Hannah entered the silent park, the early birds and squirrels scattering as her run alerted them of her presence. She had already grown winded. Her paced slowed as her chest screamed in protest. She stopped, her hands going to her knees as she bent over.

"Hannah?"

If she could have straightened at the familiar, commanding voice, she would have.

Jason's boss appeared in front of her, kneeling on the ground. "Are you all right?"

She couldn't speak, her breath gone. She shook her head.

As if she weighed nothing, Chief scooped her up into his arms and carried her to a nearby bench. Nick appeared with a bottle of water in hand beside her.

"Take a drink." Chief uncapped the bottle and shoved it into her palms.

She did and allowed her lungs to achingly fill up with air. She took another swig of the cold water.

"Better?" Nick asked.

They were both dressed in suits, both armed by the evident bulges in their jackets.

"What are you doing here?"

Chief jerked his head. "I live a few blocks away. We stopped for coffee on the way in and saw you cross the street. You're doing much better than the last time we saw you."

"Clearly not back to my old self." She scanned the area. Was it just the two of them?

"I would think it's going to take a few weeks." Nick sat next to her, his surprisingly kind eyes assessing her. "A cracked rib is no joke."

"You've been avoiding our calls." A scowl marked Chief's features as he hovered.

"I haven't taken *any* calls," she said. "Laid up, remember?"

She stood, wobbly on her feet. She needed to distance herself from these two men. The chief tossed out a hand to steady her as Nick grabbed her from behind.

"Are you sure you're all right?" Nick said, unconvinced. "You should be in the hospital."

She smacked their hands away.

"I'm fine, just out of shape and the rib clearly isn't entirely healed yet." She took a small step to her right. "They were discharging me, anyway."

"And you snuck out without allowing any of us to escort you home. What if whoever attacked you had been waiting again?" Chief said angrily. "You wouldn't have survived a second attack. We'd have to deliver the news to Jason that the woman he loved had been picked up by a coroner."

She took another step but halted. She hadn't thought of that. At the time, she only worried about sneaking away without being cornered to answer more questions and end up telling more lies and to spare Jason. Or was it herself? She couldn't even think coherently any longer. She mentally checked out of the moment she snuck away from Jason. So tired of the lies, the running, the looking over her shoulder at all times. She didn't even know who she was or what she'd become any longer.

"Hannah," Nick said. "We've come up empty. Your sketches haven't brought up any searches in the data bases we have access to."

"I think she knows that." Chief arched a brow.

She met those stark blue eyes, brandishing his wisdom.

"You have something to admit to me?" Chief said.

He knew. Undoubtedly. She slid an uneasy glance to Nick, who waited. He obviously didn't know by the expectant look on his face. Hannah stared down the Chief. What was his game? If he knew her identity, why hadn't he arrested her? Why did he stand there, waiting?

She became angry. If he wanted to go rounds, she'd play. Instead of wallowing in damn self-pity, she should get back onto her game. She broke up with Jason for a reason. To protect him from her. Meanwhile, she proceeded to curl up and hope all her problems faded away. Life didn't work that way.

Time to get back to who she knew. Who she could rely on. Who was in charge of her show.

Hannah straightened, as much as her ribs allowed, and tilted her head. She watched Chief's eyes flash, recognizing the change and challenge to come.

He gave a small shake of his head. "Don't do this, Hannah. I can help you."

She smiled shyly. "I have no idea what you're talking about."

"You may have everyone around you deceived, but I see right through you." Chief unbuttoned his jacket.

"What's going on? What did I miss?" Nick's head bounced back and forth between her and his boss.

"Jason's girl has secrets." Chief pinned her with a hard glare. "Not so little ones, either. Am I right?"

Hannah had to gain perspective. If the chief of police held any information about her in the palm of his hand, he'd have her in cuffs and in a jail cell. He might have an inkling, he may have a theory, but essentially he had zilch.

She spun on her heels, pulled her ponytail tighter, waved over her shoulder and said, "It was nice seeing both of you."

"You gonna give that diamond back to Jason?" Chief called out, freezing her in her tracks.

Her heart skipped a beat as she flicked down at the sparkly jewel. Fucking bastard knew how to get under her skin.

"It's been, what, two or three weeks since you've talked to him? You gonna keep holding on to something you keep fighting or are you gonna man up and deal?" Chief asked.

She flipped him off and jogged back toward Roy's apartment.

"I'm on your side." She heard him yell after her.

Hannah didn't know what that meant and didn't care. If she asked, that would be opening up, and if she allowed that to happen, she'd sink her own ship.

## 32

Jason popped the cap off his second beer and took a long swig. He propped his feet up on the coffee table and tried to focus on the football game. He'd been invited to watch the Monday night game at Dean's, but once again turned down his friend. Over the past three weeks, he refused any social gathering with his brothers. Hell, he hadn't visited his parents. Which meant every day his mother left him voicemail messages, expressing her concern that he hadn't stopped by or called and asking about Hannah's health. To keep her from showing up on his doorstep and assault him with a barrage of questions, he sent her a message that he remained swamped at work and Hannah was on the mend. That seemed to temporarily pacify her. Jason refused to divulge his breakup with Hannah to his parents. In reality, he had zero clue what transpired. Except Hannah no longer wanted a relationship.

He set the bottle between his thighs, his head hitting the back of the sofa. In his peripheral vision, he caught Hannah's soft sweater she constantly wore in the evenings when they'd open the windows and allow the fall air to breeze through the house. Jason snatched it, brought the material to his nose and inhaled, her scent on the piece of clothing fading.

Jason's world was empty. Lifeless. He went through the routine of his day in a state of apathy. He loathed it. Never did he dream he'd be in this shape. Not after he found the woman he wanted to spend the rest of his life with. Yeah, he'd fallen hard and fast, but so what? With every ounce of his fiber, he regarded Hannah as the one meant for him.

He pulled his phone out of his pocket and glanced at the screen, debating whether to try to call Hannah. After she threw him out of her hospital room, he gave her some space, figuring her trauma prompted a horribly rash decision. But when he unsuccessfully tried to reach her, after he found out she snuck out of the hospital and returned to her apartment to grab some clothing and hadn't been back, he gave up. Not the brightest decision, but his anger interfered with his rationale. Remorse followed, with guilt close behind. And now he held court in the lovely stage of misery. Joy.

Jason dialed Hannah's phone number and the call immediately went to voicemail. Which meant the device was turned off. Something Hannah never did. Worry rushed through his veins. He called Dean, who answered on the first ring.

"Hannah has her phone turned off," Jason blurted.

Dean sat silent for a moment. "I'm sure her battery died."

"She doesn't allow that to happen." He rose from the sofa and set the beer on the table. He shoved his feet into his running shoes.

"Why don't you come over? We can talk," Dean said.

"About?"

"Hannah."

"What about her?" Jason had his hand on the front doorknob. What did Dean want to confer with him about the woman he fell in love with, who broke his heart?

"Jason, I understand where you're coming from with Hannah. Trust me I do."

His best friend did understand. Dean had been a happily married man at one time. Jason would never forget going on that car accident call with his partner. When they pulled up, Jason knew immediately whose vehicle wrapped around that pine tree. He'd never forget the howl that came out of Dean's mouth when he jumped from their cruiser and rushed the wreckage. Which was why Dean got a pass when it came to talking to him about Hannah. His buddy appreciated that all-consuming love and loss. Jason's comparison didn't come close to the shattered man Dean became.

"Your point?"

"She told you it's over, and we need to talk about her. Chief has some suspicions you should be aware of," Dean said.

Jason heard the television and Nick and Tyler arguing in the background of the call.

"What sort of suspicions?"

"We'll talk tomorrow, unless you decide to stop by. This isn't a convo to have over the phone. Just...oh, hell, I don't know, man. I get this is killing you but break ups happen every day." The television went mute.

"She still has my ring," Jason said.

"I know, buddy."

"She hasn't returned it." Which had to mean that she continued to love him, right? That's what he repeated to himself every night he tried to sleep but couldn't, his subconscious wracked by Hannah. Where was she? Was she all right? Did she love him? Did she miss him? He really was losing his shit.

Jason opened the door and went to his car. "I'll talk to you tomorrow."

He disconnected the call, climbed into his vehicle, and drove to Hannah's. Again. Jason may not have called her recently until five minutes ago, but he sure as hell stopped by her apartment every day to see if she returned.

\*\*\*

Jason wandered aimlessly around Hannah's abandoned apartment. Searching for what, he didn't know. Two clashing sides of his psyche peppered him with their own ramblings. One hoping he found nothing. One hoping he discovered answers.

He went to the kitchen; her blender that she used to make protein shakes each morning gathered dust. The apartment windows needed cleaning from a harsh storm that passed through at the beginning of the week. He went to the bathroom to find her toiletries sat untouched on the sink. He picked up her bottle of perfume and sniffed, the same scent that lingered on the sweater more prominent to commit to memory again.

Jason went to the bedroom. Hannah's bed was neatly made, her clothes in piles where he'd left them weeks ago. Proof she hadn't returned. He swept his hand over the oak dresser and the locked trunk located at the foot of her bed. Taking it all in, his heart sank, wondering if she would ever reappear. Or was she gone for good? Hannah possessed the ability to leave everything behind without a backward glance. A trait he should have recognized and acknowledged before finding her duffle bag. Did he mean that little to her that he wasn't worth sticking around for?

Jason shut off the light and stepped into the hallway. Something flickered in his peripheral vision. His heat shot up.

A video camera.

He stood, staring at the device, in disbelief. How the hell had he not noticed the camera positioned above the bedroom door, its little round lens pointed the length of the hallway? He had an easy enough answer. The few times he walked down this area of the apartment, he focused on one thing—getting Hannah naked. She never said a word. Even when he questioned her in the hospital. She didn't give a hint that cameras existed.

If she kept that critical detail hidden, what else did she keep close to the chest? His anger stewed. His vision turned red. Rage choked him.

Jason went on a rabid search of the apartment and found cameras in the great room, the kitchen, and above the main door. All conveniently colored and ingeniously placed to blend in unless someone specifically was aware of the cameras. He also found a camera cleverly disguised as the damn gold door ornament on the outside of the apartment door. Fucking hell.

His blood boiled. Frustrated, he punched the wall. What the hell was going on?

Jason spun on his heels, taking in the apartment in a more thorough light. He did another walk through, this time focusing in on objects. Not just skimming them over as if they were part of the scenery. Like the protein shakes. Hannah worked out. A lot. Her strength for a tiny thing amazed him. Hell, he found it attractive.

He went to the coat closet and tore it apart. Nothing seemed out of the norm. He ransacked the bathroom, the linen closet, the hallway closet. Zip. He went into Hannah's bedroom and raided it, noting she owned a lot of shoes, all either flats or runners.

He spun, irate, but lost a tiny bit of his fury when he considered a reasonable possibility as to why she hadn't spoke of the cameras. Hannah might not want to admit the content of the videos in existence. They had a lot of sex, in every room, in many different ways. Jason owned every part of her delectable body. The things she allowed him to do to claim her, he'd never get with another woman. How many times had he handcuffed her to objects around the apartment and slid inside her, losing himself and taking her with him. Shame that proof of their debauchery existed most likely fueled her silence. Especially with the probability that his brothers would be the men studying those feeds. Albeit he wouldn't mind watching the videos, himself.

Focus, damn it.

Jason stood, cemented in the center of her skewed bedroom, his mind reeling. How many times had he expressed that she could tell him anything? That she could trust him. And yet she remained elusive. Closed off.

He zeroed in on the trunk and the gold padlock. The lock didn't stick out, matching the off white bedroom decor and the brown shade of the container. It coordinated with the box perfectly. Kudos to Hannah for her inventiveness. Nothing like hiding something in plain sight. What kind of fucking detective was he? And what the hell did she have in that trunk?

Jason pulled out his ever present Glock and shot right through the padlock. A neighbor would certainly call the station to report the gunfire. Soon, his brothers would show up, thinking he'd lost his mind. He couldn't disagree.

He yanked open the trunk and stared at the contents, confused. Jason knelt onto the floor and pulled out a stack of black clothing. Leggings, long sleeved black tees and workout clothes. Black socks and boots and running shoes. He found a couple small black purses as well.

Jason sank back on his heels, not understanding. Hannah wore brighter colors and they tended to be looser in fit. She liked to be comfortable. He could see her wearing form-fitted workout clothing to the gym, which she frequented, but why so much black? Women thought black made them look thinner. Did she wear the color to the gym purposely to make herself feel better? Hannah didn't need to wear the dark color. She already bordered too skinny.

He roared, annoyed. He was losing his grip on sanity. Hell, he put a bullet in a lock inside an apartment. If she did return, Hannah would be the death of him.

Depressed and downright distraught, Jason spent hours putting Hannah's apartment back together. By the time he left, after two in the morning, dreariness took hold. Jason turned one last time to view the inside of the apartment, deciding not to return. For his own stability. A deep ache and sadness riddled him. No matter what, no matter how many times he came to her apartment and wished she'd be there, she remained gone. And each time, her absence stole a piece of him. Jason understood he was wrecked and might never recover. Somehow he needed to work through his torrent of emotions. How, he didn't know. Unless Hannah changed her mind and returned to him.

## 33

Jason walked into the station, drained of all vitality. After returning from Hannah's, he went straight to bed but tossed and turned all night. Visions of her lying beside him, like he had every night for weeks, haunted him.

"Hey, buddy." Dean approached and handed him a mug of coffee.

"Thanks."

"Why don't you come to the situation room." It wasn't a suggestion by his partner.

Jason trudged behind Dean, his body and mind not wanting to focus on any case at the moment. When he entered the room, the entire detective team sat silently waiting, for him. How long had they been there? Was this some kind of brotherhood intervention? He didn't need their shit.

"Campbell." Chief nodded to the empty seat.

Jason slid into the chair, catching sight of the white board and a couple new pictures. Of Hannah. Hanging next to the pictures of their jewelry thief.

Chief pointed to the photos. "Notice a resemblance?"

Jason compared the images. He agreed their figures appeared identical, but who could really tell? The video surveillance stills captured grainy images at different angles. Not one direct or clear. But next to a picture of Hannah standing in the precinct hallway, beside Chief, the physical outline resemblance was remarkable. That meant nothing to Jason.

"So their bodies could pass as similar," Jason said.

Nick jumped in. "She gave us false sketches," he said. Nick's obvious sympathy for him grated on Jason's nerves. "The artist knew it immediately."

"She snuck out of the hospital," Tyler said.

Jason's temperature rose. His blood pressure taking a hit as of late. What the hell was this? They were trying to put the blame of the robberies on Hannah? *His* Hannah? Who wouldn't know the first thing about breaking into a jewelry store. Until recently, she held down a decent full time job. Well, as far as he knew. "She left the hospital to avoid facing all of you. Do you know how humiliating it must be for her? She got the crap beat out of her in a place she was supposed to be safe. Her home."

"After which she disappeared," Chief said.

"We fucking broke up." Jason pounded his fist off the table. "What the hell is this? Are you all insane? You're grasping for straws. You're hell bent on catching this thief so you don't have to call in the feds. Well, fuck you all. You know Hannah didn't do this. She couldn't have. For fuck's sake, I combed her house last night and found nothing."

"Nothing?" Nick raised a brow.

"Nothing. I searched closets, drawers, even her damn trunk at the bottom of her bed."

"Why did you decide to go through her home?" Dean asked.

Jason opened his mouth and shut it, like an idiot. Shit, in his anger, he mistakenly spilled about his tirade. What the hell did he say? That he had thought along the same lines as them for a brief moment last night? That his lack of better judgment got to him, trying to find any valid reason, other than the inconsistencies Hannah gave him, for her to drop him like a bad habit? No, that'd only flame their suspicion.

"What do you know, Campbell?" Chief braced his hands on the large conference table. "Spill."

The cameras meant nothing. Just because she had them didn't mean guilt for anything plagued her, other than hiding their sexcapades. At last that's what his heart alleged.

"Jason," Nick coaxed.

"I found cameras." That damn loyal cop in him consistently took over when he found himself split in two. Even over the slightest thing. Why the hell would he throw Hannah under the bus by confessing what he found? God, he hated himself.

Chief turned to Tyler. "Try to get a warrant for those cameras."

"But we have nothing to garner a warrant." Tyler didn't bother to hide his disappointment.

Chief stared Jason down. He slammed his fist against the white board, the pictures flying at the force, the black markers dropping to the floor. "Damn it."

"Why the hell do you want to prove this thief is Hannah?" Jason growled, the protective boyfriend in him finally deciding to make an appearance. "For your own fucking enjoyment?"

"She's not who you think she is." Chief's arrogance and finality illustrated his hardened viewpoint of Hannah. "I gave her the opportunity to help her but she turned her back on us. She's the perp."

"She is not your fucking thief," Jason bellowed. The temperature in the room turned cold, a standoff between a chief and his detective about to go down.

Nick stood and held out his hands. "Let's calm down."

"Everyone will stay on top of McIntyre's. We haven't heard from Hannah in weeks. If those men who attacked her are after money, they didn't visit and put a hurting on her for chump change. Which means she'll be desperate to get her hands onto a large amount of cash and quickly." Chief managed to go from Hannah being the thief to a conspiracy of thugs and money, with no proof.

Jason sprang from his chair, it flying back and hitting the floor. "I won't stand here and let you do this to her. I fucking love her. That's the woman I want to spend the rest of my life with and this is how you treat her without questioning her?"

"She disappeared before we could, rendering us to come up with our own theories," Tyler said.

"How well do you think you know that woman?" Dean asked.

"Fuck off." Jason hurled open the door and stormed out of the room.

He pulled out his cell and dialed Hannah as he stalked out to his car. When her voicemail picked up, again, he left a message. "Hannah, I need you to call me immediately. We're in a bit of trouble."

Hannah played Jason's message for Roy, knowing what her friend would say. He'd just shown her the video of Jason finding the cameras and tearing apart her place. They both about had a heart attack when he opened her trunk. Thank goodness she grabbed the pouch with diamonds and bag of cash when she'd come back for her clothes.

Her heart sank at the knowledge that without a doubt, her relationship with Jason ended. For weeks, a glimmer of hope they might be able to work out their issues—specifically her illegal complexities— kept her going. But now he'd never trust her and truth be told, she couldn't be trusted with someone as honorable as Jason.

"He knows. We need to abandon this heist." Roy wore a hole the carpet of his cramped living room space.

"I know we should," she said. "But the issue is the mob found me and they'll find me wherever I go. I need to get them this money. After I do, I'll go to Carl and ask for help."

"You're just going to end up trading one shady character for another. Which one is the lesser of two evils?" Roy slumped down in his chair. "If you pay this money they want recouped, because they can't find your parents, who's to say they'll be satisfied this time? The mob now wants your parents, even if you reimburse their losses. It's simple business to them. Revenge. Your parents crossed a line by robbing the boss's home. I would guess the reason they're here is that they've exhausted their search capabilities within the US. *You* are their last resort and gateway to finding your loser parents. With the threat of killing you, and your will to live, they get their money and bet that you'll search for your parents, leading the sharks straight to the meat they want to consume. I'd assume that's their thought process. Who can know for sure?"

"This is beyond payment." She stared out the apartment window to the street below, noting the large cracks in the concrete sidewalk, wondering how just a month ago her life seemed perfect. Not a crack in the immaculate surface. But now it was a big old cluster fuck. "This is my parents stealing from a man you don't take from. This time I will end up dead before my parents if I don't pay."

Hot tears stung her eyes. An early grave didn't top her to-do list. All she could envision was Jason's devastation when called to identify her body. *If* they ever found her remains. Roy couldn't do it. He'd die trying to step through the doorway to his apartment. And he would desperately give it his best effort.

"Hannah," Roy said. "Let's just go. You can knock me out with meds and we'll drive somewhere. The desert?"

"Great place to hide a body."

"The mountains?"

"Great place to have mountain lions eat a body."

"Near the ocean?"

"Sharks."

Roy exhaled, clearly at his wits end with her. "You're going to do this with or without me, aren't you?"

"Yes," she said. "I have to. But I need your help. Please don't turn your back on me."

Roy glared. "I'm offended you'd say those words out loud."

"Sorry."

"Everything about this one is going to have to be perfect. From the date, time, weather. Everything." Roy swiveled in his chair and pulled up the interior floor plans for McIntyre's. How he got them, Hannah had no clue. He probably hacked a server that no mortal could get into. His online technical degree paid off in spades. Well, for her benefit.

She ambled over next to her best friend, pulled up a chair, and dropped into the seat. The staggering sense of loss weighed her down. "I love him."

"I know." Roy remained engrossed on the computer screen.

"I never thought I'd love someone."

"I know."

A single tear slid down her cheek. "I wasn't meant to be with someone. This is the life I was meant to live."

"I don't believe that for one second." Roy clicked away on his computer. He slanted her a considering stare. "If that was the case, you wouldn't have met Jason."

Surprised, Hannah didn't realize Roy bought into fate. But more astonishing was his hidden admission that he wished the best for her and he thought that included Jason. She'd thought so, as well. Too bad her life consisted of shitty parents who laid their troubles on her doorstep and the mob who deemed it necessary to collect their money.

"Carl can help you," Roy said. "We have to speculate door number two has better fortuity behind it."

He was probably trying to give her a sliver of hope. Something she couldn't afford to have at the moment. She needed precise results and outcomes. Hope walked the same line as wishing. Might as well flip a coin into a well, spin around three times, and watch for falling stars.

"Doubtful."

Hannah dropped the subject, not wanting to debate Carl or Jason. Their attention needed to be fixated on more important issues at hand.

\*\*\*

"Can you get me a motorcycle?" Hannah asked.

Carl raised a brow, probably shocked by her forceful tone. "Do you know how to ride a bike?"

She shrugged. "How hard can it be?"

He barked out a laugh. "Are you suicidal?"

"Every day."

Carl's smile vanished. "Something's wrong. What is it?"

Hannah shook her head, unwilling to disclose her predicament. "I can't get into that right now. After this next one, I do need to have a one-on-one with you."

He sat forward, his chair straining with a creak, and leaned on his desk. "Hannah, if there's an issue, you should tell me."

Hannah still hadn't come to a personal agreement whether or not to ask Carl for help. After weighing

Roy's words, he was correct. She would be trading one cunning mobster for another. She had an idea of what to expect with her parents' cohorts. She could forge a shield of defense and give herself a fighting chance. Carl remained a mystery, only knowing that he paid her fairly. She did no other business with him and he never approached her for any type of services, other than when she came to him to get rid of diamonds.

"I will."

He repressed a smile. "Women."

A couple of the men in the room snickered. Carl beckoned to one of the guys. "See about getting her a bike. I'm assuming a quiet crotch rocket?"

"Is there such a thing?"

"No." He grinned deviously.

Hannah followed one of the men out of the room but turned before she stepped past the threshold. "It wouldn't be such a bad thing if your men happened to be in the neighborhood of McIntyre's Thursday night, around one or so?"

Carl raised a brow, sat back, and tapped a forefinger over his bottom lip. "Overreaching?"

"Always."

"That's a dangerous one."

"I'm aware."

"Are you?"

She spun back around and tipped her head, challenging him. "Are you suggesting I don't know what I'm doing? You've cashed in a hell of a lot of money off me."

"Close the door. Everyone out." Carl's back went ramrod straight and his eyes flared black as night.

Damn it, she pressed her luck.

The men scattered, leaving her alone with a very dangerous man.

"Sit." He pointed to the chair opposite his desk.

She did as instructed.

"First, don't give me shit. I respect the hell out of you. You seem to have a good head on your shoulders, don't play games, and aren't crazy as fuck. A rarity in my world. So when I ask you a question, specifically to make certain you're all right, I expect an answer with a modicum of mutual respect." Carl's features turned to wall of stone. Blank. Even his tone didn't rise or fall. Hannah favored yelling, that type of communication far less frightening.

"Do you know you're playing a dangerous game with McIntyre's?"

"That's why I mentioned about visiting that part of town." Exhaustion crept up. Her health continued to be less than one hundred percent, say about ninety-five, moments of fatigue continuing to settle in. Probably more mental than actual physical.

"And I will make certain my men happen to be in the area, but why this one?" His gaze drilled into hers.

"I don't have a choice."

"We all have choices. You might not like your options but there are always choices." He sat back, relaxing. A man without worry or fear. Someone in total control at all times. "I'm offering you my help. If you don't want to tell me why you're choosing this store, of all the shops available, I can't force you to. But I'm going to throw in my two cents. Walk away."

She was offended by the suggestion. "Are you saying I can't do this job?"

"Oh, I know you can do it, but at what price?"

Hannah didn't respond. What price wouldn't she pay to get out of her parents' grip? What was the price for self-preservation?

\*\*\*

Hannah straddled the bike she'd been joy riding for the past couple days. Her car safely hidden in Carl's compound, he allowed her to drive off with the sexy form of transportation. He had appreciated her glee when she straddled the machine. She'd spent more time whizzing around Pittsburgh at insane speeds than actually doing leg work for her heist. Now Roy glared down at her from his window as she drove off, fifteen minutes behind schedule.

Hannah flew down the dark streets, the night still and ominous with a half moon covered by clouds. For the last three weeks, the weather had been dry and warm for October. Naturally mother nature figured a light sprinkle on the roads would help challenge Hannah. The bitch.

After twenty minutes of making certain law enforcement didn't find her and have a tail on her, a normal routine with every job, she parked her new shiny toy five blocks away from her target, behind an abandoned building. That storefront used to house a pharmacy, a book store, and a restaurant. Its emptiness now blended into the background. A perfect rendezvous point for herself to make a quick, unseen getaway.

Hannah took off her black helmet, opened the storage compartment and pulled out her mask and quickly hid her identity, a tool kit Roy contrived for her, her phone, and hip bag. For this take, she needed more equipment, all which intended to be left behind. She spent hours scrubbing the pieces clean of any remarkable evidence.

She dialed Roy's number, which he answered on the first ring. "I'm here."

"Please be careful."

"I will."

He refused to be totally on board with this plan. Even as she left his apartment, he tried to talk her out of this robbery. Hannah lovingly patted him on the head and informed him by next week they'd be starting over somewhere else. A beach on the coast of Florida. Roy had cursed under his breath about her stubbornness.

Hannah locked her phone so the line wouldn't disconnect and placed it into her secure armband. She scooted her way to McIntyre's by becoming one with the brick walls of the buildings she crept past. The slight rain annoyed her, hindering her ability to listen for unusual racket, footsteps, or approaching vehicles. Her cautionary progression was slower than her usual steady pace due to the inclement weather.

Her target lit up the night, its bright sign in the front, a beacon calling to her. Her object within her grasp. Hannah's blood pumped as she breathed in through her nose and out her mouth to keep herself calm. Finally the high from her rush of adrenaline peaked. Light on her toes, her vision cleared and the rain disappeared. There was nothing but her and the jewelry store. A small hurdle to get her free from the man who wanted payback for the theft of objects from his home.

Hannah lay in wait behind the family-owned craft store next to McIntyre's. She scoped her surroundings, scouting for anything out of the norm, and zeroed in on the electrical box at the back of the building. Precisely where Roy said it'd be located.

When all was clear, she scurried to the back of the building, making quick work of pulling out the tools, opening the box, and putting the clamp thingy with a small black box attached on the appropriate set of wires. She waited for the lights on the box to turn green. She knew Roy currently sat behind his computer to disarm the entrance alarms and she had to wait for the all clear. But it seemed to take longer than she anticipated. Way too long. She glanced at her watch. One minute past the allotted time. She scanned the area again, taking note of the camera perched directly above the box, positioned right down upon her. A perfect shot of her obscured form. Her heart rate spiked. Her palms started to sweat inside her gloves. She jerked her head downward, afraid of any chance of detection. She'd be remiss to deny she grew nervous when up close and personal with cameras. Roy took great care to keep her identity hidden but mistakes could happen.

She took quick stock in herself, making certain every inch of her body remained covered. Blowing out a couple calming breaths, she slowed her pulse. No need to get worked up and cause undue stress.

When the lights finally blinked green, she went to the backdoor of the building located to the right of the box, pulled out her toolkit to dislodge the steel door. This was the very reason she worked tirelessly at the gym. Weakness wouldn't get her through the heavy steel. She needed her strength to pry open the door after she used the specially designed equipment to disengage the bolts and electrical lock to dislodge the structure. It would be sealed shut, needing a firm tug.

Hannah yanked open the door and slinked inside the storage room, her back plastered against the wall. When she did a job, she never appreciated the fact that it normally encompassed a quick in and out game. This time the entire scene conjured an out of body experience. As if watching a 3-D action flick that, as a spectator, she could discern every movement and hold of breath. She didn't like the sensation. A twinge of dread crossed over her. She rapidly squashed that reaction. She didn't have time to dwell on morality or dangerous possibilities.

Hannah waited for her phone to glint green, giving her the okay to move throughout the storage room after Roy hacked the video surveillance. She carefully moved about, aware of the guards on duty performing their rounds. She glanced at her watch as she slid to the door that led to the first floor show room. According to Roy's calculations, a guard would be exiting the floor in thirty seconds. She watched the second hand on her ten dollar watch count down. The irony not lost on her.

She listened to her surroundings, noting the air conditioning didn't run on the unseasonably warm day. Roy, who managed to seize control of the entire store from his laptop at his apartment, shut it down so she could hear a feather drop.

At the thirty second mark, Hannah slowly opened the door and slithered into the dimly lit showroom. She flattened herself against the wall, taking in her surroundings. She became a ghost, blending into the background. She shimmied her way to the stairwell and quietly climbed the steps to the second level where the loose jewels were displayed. This area housed the priceless jewelry created by the artists.

Hannah stealthily inched her way to the flawless diamond display case. There would be no smash and grab tonight. Too many guards. Seven, to be precise. Two inside performing rounds. Three outside casing the perimeter. Two in the video surveillance room. The two cramped in the room the size of a closet both received porn emails on their smart phones that sent their devices into a wall of spam five minutes before she arrived. A very nice distraction by her Roy. He planned to play a recorded surveillance video on a loop.

A suitable cutting of the glass needed to occur. She vaulted behind the case, crouched down, and pulled the cutter out of her bag. She didn't have time to search for keys to the locked displays.

It only took her a couple minutes to make a small, perfectly round hole to fit her hand through and snatch all the precious diamonds available. Next, she fixated on the rubies and repeated the process. Lastly, maneuvering to the pearls. She focused in on her project while also keeping a watchful eye. Not many people knew how to multitask two important duties to keep themselves not only on their game, but aware of potential danger. She spent hours training herself for such missions. And that's what this was to her. A mission to rid herself of further surprise visits and beatings, to extract herself from her parents dragging her down with them, of a shallow grave. A pursuit to never fall into the world she grew up in—poor, hungry, desolate. She would succeed.

Once Hannah had all the items she needed, which turned out to be more than she anticipated and would bring her in greater money that she originally figured, she tiptoed her way back down the steps to exit the same way entered. Everything had gone according to plan. She could count the seconds to bidding farewell to the city.

"Stop!" a deep voice bellowed from behind. "Put your hands up."

Hannah stopped and glanced over her right shoulder. One of the security guards must have been on the ball to complete his rounds early. Surprise.

She slowly raised her hands in mock surrender. Something she had no intention of ever doing.

"Get down on the ground."

Really? So boring. Her blood pulsed rapidly through her veins. A familiar need to challenge and dance enveloped her. That piece of her she loved to embrace, but had stamped down while with Jason. Not that she'd needed it then. She'd managed to go straight while they'd been together for that brief period.

Hannah spun, facing down a very large stun gun, thankful he didn't pull a firearm on her. She grinned, not that he'd see through her full face mask.

"I said get down on the ground."

She slowly, dramatically shook her head. She needed him to approach her. He didn't disappoint.

The guard stalked closer and she waited until he edged within arm's reach before dropping to the ground, kicking forward, and taking his legs out from underneath him. The fool should have pulled the trigger further back. He discharged the weapon, not even close to connecting to her.

She followed up with a swift kick to the balls and punch to his temple, knocking him out cold. Too easy. Which didn't set well with her. She needed to get out of the building. Now.

Hannah spun and raced for the back door to exit the store. She managed to get outside the building and down a block. And then all hell broke loose.

## 35

"Stop!" Jason pointed his weapon straight at the perp's back. Tyler stepped out of the shadow of the brick building and had her front covered. "Put your hands up where I can see them."

Slowly she raised her hands in surrender.

"We've got the perp outside. Two blocks east behind the paint store," Jason reported into his shoulder radio. A full head mask covered her features but that body, that hourglass shape, up close and personal, his heart sank into his stomach. Please, please don't tell him his Hannah stood with her back to him, stolen diamonds in that hip bag. A replica of the one in the trunk that sat at the end of her bed.

Tyler took a step closer to her.

"Tyler," he warned. How he managed to end up with Tyler as his partner this evening, he didn't know. But keeping an eye on the overzealous detective as well as apprehending their perp wasn't something he prepared for.

"Get down on your knees." Jason kept his gun pointed her direction, despite his inner turmoil and three fold duty of supervising Tyler, arresting their perp, and praying that wasn't Hannah.

At first she didn't move, but he saw the subtle shake of her body. A slow, musical laugh filled the night air. A vaguely familiar melody.

Fuck, fuck, fuck. This wasn't happening. His brothers couldn't have been right. His chief had to be wrong. Sweat dripped down his forehead, stinging his eyes.

"Get. Down. On. Your. Knees." He gritted his teeth, angry at her defiance. He wasn't playing around. He needed to unmask this thief and prove his team wrong.

She glanced over her shoulder and he could literally feel her eyes burrow into him through that cover up. She spoke low and slowly, obviously disguising her voice. "I can't do that."

He tilted his head as his stomach flipped. Jason took a deep breath, maintaining the composure that had been ingrained into him from the academy and years on the force. He couldn't allow his devastation at the possibility that Hannah might be under that get-up to effect him. He had a job to do.

Jason took a couple steps closer. She was small, five foot and a few inches. His law enforcement training and his personal intrigue dueled inside him to make an arrest and get answers.

Before he took another step, Tyler grew frustrated and took matters into his own hands and went after her in a tackle lunge.

Fucking hell, the kid watched too much television and had no patience.

In a quick movement he'd only seen professional fighters and military use, she out-maneuvered Tyler, who bypassed her, trying to gain his balance before face-planting to the asphalt. She managed a swift kick to Tyler's nuts as she spun away from him and followed with a devastating kick to the back of his thigh. A loud crunch cracked the night.

A piercing scream bounced off the alley behind the dark buildings.

Jason rushed toward her, unwilling to use his weapon since she appeared unarmed. Except for her cat-like reflexes and trained defensive moves.

Their thief fled the scene. Her short legs ate up distance quickly. Jason pursued until the night erupted with a gunshot, the loud blast echoing off the back of the buildings.

Jason ducked and threw himself against the brick of the building, his weapon pointed at the suspect. Where the hell had that shot come from? Was it her entourage? He scanned the area, going from their suspect to his partner. Tyler lay on his back, his gun pointed the direction of the escaping perp. He shot off another round.

"Tyler!"

Jason's gaze swung back to the thief, whose pace had slowed, now two blocks away and rounding the corner between the buildings. He took off after her again. If he didn't catch up, she might disappear on him.

He sprinted to the main street and found her rushing across the road, almost three blocks ahead. She suddenly stopped, dropped to her knees, and clutched her back. Two blocks away. She pushed off the ground and stumbled to her feet. Her motions now jerky.

Twenty feet from catching her and his world tumbled. Her black shirt rode up, exposing her skin, revealing a familiar tramp stamp. A horoscope symbol. One that most might mistake as the letter H. On the right side of her back, a bullet wound, blood running down and disappearing into her black pants.

Jason's mind went blank. Everything he knew came to a grinding halt. He stopped, unable to move. A nightmare. He had to be having a nightmare. He'd wake up and Hannah would be asleep curled up against him, naked. All of this a horrid dream.

"Hannah?" he called out.

Only the slightest falter in her step occurred as she lumbered away.

Out of nowhere, a nondescript van with blacked out windows squealed down the side street. A side door opened as Hannah floundered toward the van. Jason found his footing and raced to get to her. It would be a matter of perfect timing to nab her before she disappeared forever. He couldn't let her get away.

Jason missed her by a hair's breath as she jumped into the van, two men dressed in black from head to toe, yanking her inside by her clothing. He chased after the vehicle for only a few feet to see the van had no license. Naturally.

His chest heaved, trying to get air into his lungs. Pain developed in his head and at the center of his chest. And it had nothing to do with lack of oxygen.

## 36

"She needs a surgeon, Derrick," Carl said to someone in the room.

Hannah kept going in and out of consciousness. How long had she been doing that? Days? Weeks? She writhed at the burning pain streaming throughout her body.

"She needs blood," another voice said.

"Who is she?" a smooth, calm voice said.

"She's my jewel supplier."

"*She* is the one the police cannot catch?" the unknown voice said.

"Yes," Carl answered.

"Impressive."

Their conversation, as if she didn't have a gunshot wound to her back, annoyed the hell out of her. She wanted to scream for them to get out. Or better yet, get her some fucking help. Was she dying? Was it this excruciating crossing over? Was this her drawn out, torturous end? All for the sake of some pieces of hard rock that sold for a mint?

Her head drooped to the side. A brightly lit room pierced her eyes, making her squint. Men she recognized from Carl's office surrounded her. Concern etched their faces. Which didn't help to comfort her.

A man in scrubs approached her. "I'm going to give you something to knock you out. I need to get the bullet out of you, okay."

"'Kay," she croaked through the searing pain. Soon she lost sensation in her legs and arms. Did the bullet hit her spine? With luck like that, she wanted a refund.

Carl stepped up next to her. "Who shot you, baby girl? Which cop was it?"

Averting her gaze, she refused to answer. She knew Tyler pulled the trigger, but couldn't place blame for doing his job. Only one person could take any credit for her condition and she happened to be lying in a pool of her own blood.

Hannah's eyes grew heavy and the room began to spin in a vertical direction. The horror written across Jason's features at the realization of who his thief turned out to be assaulted her right before she fell under the spell of the drugs. She tried to call out Jason's name but her voice wouldn't cooperate.

\*\*\*

How long had she been out? When she blinked her eyes open, a beautiful brown-haired, blue-eyed little girl stared down at her.

"She's awake!" The little girl's high pitched tone rang through her eardrums. A blinding pounding pulsed through her skull.

Hannah found herself in a plain bedroom. White walls, tan curtains, and a single chest of drawers. She lay on a queen-sized bed with white sheets and bedding to match the curtains. She supposed the pillow her head rested on might be soft, not an actual stack of bricks.

Carl entered the room with a stunningly handsome man behind him—tall with dark brown hair and dressed in a designer suit. His chocolate brown eyes honed in on her.

"Caitlin, I told you not to disturb her," the man scolded.

"I was only watching her breathe, Daddy," the little girl said factually.

"Thank you for keeping an eye on her. Now go find your brother and keep an eye on him." The girl skipped out of the room as her father gently touched the top of her head when she passed by him. Why the hell would he bring his daughter to her bedside?

Carl approached her left side. "Hannah, this is my boss, Derrick Murphy. He's the one who called the doctor to treat you last night."

Only one night she'd been out?

Hannah's hazy gaze bounced between the two men.

Derrick smoothly slid onto the edge of the bed. "I admit, I am impressed. But I do have a question. Why?"

Why what?

She squirmed under Mr. Murphy's hard study and winced at the minor shift. Her body ached something fierce. She never experienced this type of discomfort. She couldn't pinpoint the pain accurately enough, but her brain focused in on the injury and swaddled itself around the agony.

"How are you feeling?" Carl asked.

"Tired," she said. "My head and body are killing me."

"I'll get you a pain pill. You'll stay here for a few days where the doc can check on you." He limped out of the room.

"I can't take pain meds."

The gorgeous man's eyes narrowed. "You will."

She went to argue but he glared menacingly. She clamped her mouth shut. Where the hell was she?

"You're upstairs at Carl's office." He picked up a glass of water and helped her to take a drink.

"You need the pain medication for your body to relax. We cannot have your wound opening back up." Mr. Murphy uncannily answered both her unasked questions and also shut down her meds refusal.

"What is your position?"

Mr. Murphy grinned and gently helped her lay back.

"Why, you have never heard of me?" He was mocking her.

Carl came back into the room, his leg making his movements slow. He handed her a pill and helped her with a second drink of water, which she emptied the remainder, her throat dry. It tasted like heaven.

"Carl, leave us." Mr. Murphy's command gave no room for argument.

Mr. Murphy lifted his chin toward the door Carl closed behind him. "Carl's limp?"

Hannah always wondered how he came into that hobble but never had the balls to ask. Was Mr. Murphy going to randomly address the topic with her? Odd. Why? But she remained too frightened and physically vulnerable to spit out any of her attitude.

"My brother did that to him." Derrick swept her hair off her forehead. "You're warm. I'll make sure the doctor gets here quickly. We don't want you to develop an infection." He unbuttoned his navy blue jacket.

"Before my brother died, he was the head of my family. He was a man not to be reckoned with. When I took his position years ago, I expanded his original operation throughout the Northeast into an untouchable enterprise. My reach knows no bounds. I happen to know the business of jewelry robbery. Not really my forte, but I know it. Women do not get into heisting jewelry stores unless there is a specific reason. Women have an ingrained morality that keeps them from choosing the lifestyle you have. Only those desperate to pull themselves out of a situation turn to the life of crime you have brilliantly committed. Heisting a store is a quick way to obtain cash. Diamonds and gems need to be sold on the street in order to make money. Why do you need the money, Hannah?" His inarguable perception floored her.

Holy hell, not only gorgeous, but intelligent, as well.

She closed her eyes in a long blink. Did she confess to him why? What did she do in a situation like this? Only Roy knew her reasons for choosing her way of life.

"Don't you dare fall asleep on me when I have asked you a question." His tone was unyielding.

Her lids flew open.

"What do you have to lose? Could there be an off chance I can help you?" His hard features softened only slightly. But she knew his type. No matter what she confessed to Mr. Murphy, he remained a mob boss. Apparently a very powerful one. Did she continue going through door number one? Or did she finally open door number two and hope for a better result?

Hannah took a leap of faith. When she finished explaining her plight, Mr. Murphy said nothing for an uncomfortably long moment.

"I can help you out of this situation," he said. "But it comes at a price."

Indeed it did.

"Your parents will now be held directly responsible with their own lives." He waved to her current state. "So before I make a phone call to put a stop to these men from  coming after you again, determine right now if you can handle the fact that your parents will end up paying the ultimate price. Likely sooner rather than later. If I do not make that call, I cannot help your situation."

Her mind a haze, she tried to rationally consider her options. Carl said to her she always had a choice. That decision right now held her shitty parents' lives in her hands. Did she tell Mr. Murphy to forget it and keep living a life on the run, robbing jewelry stores and potentially getting shot again? Or did she take his offer and finally start trying to build a normal life? Try to redeem herself and her sins. Did she release Roy of his constant anxiety over her and his accomplice status? All of it may be a moot point since the police, specifically Jason, now knew the identity of their thief.

"If I say yes to your offer, I have a bigger issue at hand."

He raised a brow. "A larger issue than lying in a bed, recovering from a gunshot wound?"

"The police know who I am."

He chuckled, as if that news meant nothing. What the hell, she could go to jail. "Trust me, I'll take care of that small blip. Carl's ass is on the line, too. I cannot have my right hand man behind bars. He brings too much money into the fold."

Mr. Murphy leaned down and whispered into her ear. "I will make the call and will pull strings to deal with the police. Again, at a price."

She groaned, not liking that statement. Roy was right, she just traded one shady character for another.

"Don't worry. It could be something as simple as babysitting my children." He stood, turned and left the room, chuckling evilly.

"Daddy, can I visit the woman in the bed?" Hannah heard the young girl in the hallway.

"Caitlin, the woman in the bed is ill. Leave her be. And I told you to play with your brother." Their voices faded as they got further from the bedroom and Hannah's eyelids gave up the battle to remain open.

Even as she once again succumbed to the darkness, Jason's handsome image appeared, her heart plummeting over her loss.

## 37

Every day for three weeks Jason visited Hannah's apartment, using his key to gain access to her place. And every single day, no sign that she returned to her apartment seemed evident. Meanwhile, his world fell apart at the seams. He couldn't sleep or eat. He didn't function at work. Jason didn't know whether Hannah was alive or dead. Chief had a complete meltdown over Tyler shooting their suspect and of the suspect injuring his detective. Tyler, sporting a full leg cast, had months of recovery ahead of him. They were now down one detective on the team. Of course all his brothers wholeheartedly asserted Hannah, their unidentified thief, assaulted their brother and managed to escape.

No one knew exactly what happened the evening they cased McIntyre's, including Jason. They'd had their perp within their grasp but it'd all gone to hell. Tyler could be blamed for the initial fuck up. And Chief did say he would be reprimanded. Tyler's obsession with bringing their thief to justice managed to trump his by-the-book mentality.

But when Jason should have taken over, he'd lost all sense of duty. He'd been betrayed. Every word Chief and Dean and his brothers said had been true. Hannah was the jewelry thief. That knowledge did more than rankle Jason, it destroyed him.

Was all of Hannah's words, her admissions, her love, a lie? Did she use him for information regarding the case?

Surely she had. Why the hell else would she have been with him? Worse, when he recalled their initial contact, he had approached her. What an asshat. She made him into a fool.

But he kept that all to himself. He struggled with the knowledge he possessed. The cop in him wanted to lay it all out on the table and allow his brothers to move forward. The man who'd fallen so deep and so hard couldn't imagine turning over the woman who ensnared his heart. Hell, he couldn't even go to his parents, spill his guts, and get some sort of helpful advice. As he held paperwork to be signed, going over the details of the incident, he pulled up his email account to compare the outline sent that morning. It occurred to Jason he'd been subconsciously protecting Hannah. A small part of him held out hope all of their theories were wrong. That a doppelganger canvassed the city at night, heisting jewelry stores, toying with law enforcement.

God, he hoped she was alive and recovering somewhere safe. He tried every lead he knew to find her. He searched every nook and cranny in her apartment but found nothing. Her cell phone had been clearly shut down. His fellow LEO brother on a task force came up with no pings when he searched the number. Hell, Jason didn't even know how to contact this Roy guy. Fucking hell. He knew next to nothing about Hannah and his anger at that fact consumed him, threatening to crawl into his gut and eat away at him inside out. He had no idea how cagey his Hannah could be.

He scrolled through the group email sent by Nick and went over the notes. Jason's silence and lack of forthcoming left substantial holes of the night open. Everything he'd ever been taught and trained thrown out the window. He glanced up at the Chief's office. He could easily go in there and admit about the tattoo, the items he found in Hannah's trunk, and the fact she reacted when he called out her name. But Jason, without a doubt, knew that as soon as that happened, he'd never see Hannah again and would always be tormented by the question, why?

Was the story about her parents true? And her job description, how deceptively wordy to describe being a talented jewelry thief.

Damn it. Not only livid, Jason's head remained confused and his heart broken. He'd asked her to marry him. She said yes. He wanted to settle down with Hannah and start a family. Create a life together. Turned out the woman he loved was nothing but a figment of what he wanted, ingeniously played by her.

Jason slammed his fist off his desk, items bouncing at the forceful vibrations.

He'd introduced her to his parents. She briefly rubbed elbows with his partner and the entire force. The guys actually liked her and approved. That is, until his detective brothers got it into their heads she might be their criminal.

"What's got you all riled up?" Dean approached, a stack of paperwork in his hands. They were all up to their necks in forms and signatures as a result of the night gone wrong.

"Nothing," he mumbled.

"Right," Dean said. "You've been walking around here a miserable fuck for three weeks. Since the night our girl got away."

Jason eyed him over his the travel mug he picked up and took a sip out of. He spit out the day old coffee. Where was his partner leading him?

"I have a theory."

Great.

"Talked to Tyler. He said after he shot the girl, you chased her. You're a pretty quick guy. In fact, your running speed is quite fast for a big man. Our thief is short, which means her legs are as well. Now, she can be fast, but math says that you'd catch up with her. Which means, in my humble opinion, and knowing you quite well, something happened and you let her go." Dean was too close to the truth for Jason's liking. "And only one thing could do that to a cop. You know her. And you just don't know her, that wouldn't matter to any officer. At some point, we all arrest someone we know. She's the woman you asked to marry you. *That* would be the one thing to throw any one of us off."

Jason didn't answer. He didn't want to lie to his longtime partner. But until he talked to and found out for certain that their suspect was, in fact, Hannah, he refused to acknowledge any assumption. He recognized his desperate grasp at straws.

"I can't begin to tell you if she is or isn't. I didn't get to see her face. No one has. So as far as we all know, she could be anyone." Jason picked up his fresh mug of caffeine.

Dean smirked and shook his head. He leaned in close. "I wouldn't give her up either if I were you. We can't control who we fall in love with and what happens after we hand that woman our heart. It would be so much easier to shut down and walk away. Move on. But that's not the way a man works."

Jason straightened. Sympathy for his best friend, who'd single handedly had his world collapse in a split second car accident, wedged into his overabundance of emotions.

"Keep this in mind, if she is the thief, she wrecked Tyler. Can you trust her not to put a bullet into your back or the back of the head of your partner?" Dean said.

"Tyler went after her first when he shouldn't have." Jason's gritty defense unmistakable. "He jeopardized the entire mission. We would have had her cuffed and in jail."

"Do you really think she would have allowed the two of you to take her in? You don't know if she wasn't armed. When she broke Tyler's leg, she just didn't have the opportunity to pull out a weapon." Dean set his stack of papers aside on his own desk. "Unfortunately the video surveillance from every single shop in that area conveniently went dark for a half an hour. No getaway vehicle identification. Nothing to give us a hint of where she might have been headed. We can't study video to say whether or not she was or was not armed. We have nothing to back up Tyler's story of being attacked. The only jackpot of the night was finding that motorcycle. But that has come up empty, the bike was wiped clean."

"You weren't there, you have no idea what actually went down. She had plenty of time to pull out a gun, knife, hell even a firecracker and light it up and send it flying. She wasn't armed because she's not violent." His lips twitched into a snarl, his frustration growing.

"But she is, hence Tyler's immobile condition." Dean laid a supportive hand on his shoulder. "Hey man, I know this has you fucked up. If it was me, I'd be the same way. Hell, I like Hannah a lot. But let's say for argument's sake she is the perp, what the hell are you going to do?"

"I don't know." Jason slumped back in his chair, his combativeness fizzing out. "I don't even know if she's alive. I'm scared to death she's dead and I'll never know."

Dean squeezed his shoulder. "So it was her."

Jason's head hit his hands. Goddamn Dean. His partner dug deeper than most to get the answers he wanted. Jason couldn't fault him. He would do the same if the roles were reversed.

His partner shook his head. "You don't have to answer. I won't do that to you. It's up to you to come clean. If you need anything, let me know. I'll help you any way I can. You've had my back more times than I'll ever be able to repay in our lifetimes. Just remember this, you're a cop first. You took an oath to do the right thing at all times."

In a moment he never dreamed would occur, Jason questioned his commitment to his career. He could practically see the fork in the road ahead. Never would he have thought the upheaval of his world could be induced by a woman he'd fallen in love with.

Dean slapped him on the back, pushed off the desk and went to the common area. When his gaze swung to the Chief's office, his boss stood with his arms crossed over his chest, staring Jason's direction through the large window.

Jason recognized that scowl. Chief knew Jason's game. He knew Jason allowed the woman he loved to escape, compromising him, the unit, and the precinct. The feds had been breathing down Chief's neck for the past three weeks, wanting inside their house. But Chief refused to welcome them. Everyone knew why. Their house didn't exactly have clean closets. More than one member of the police force had something to hide. Deep down, all were genuinely decent members of the community and good law enforcement professionals, and their chief protected each man and woman on staff. Jason had to wonder if Chief was one of those with a skeleton.

\*\*\*

Jason pulled out his keys and unlocked the door to Hannah's apartment. Again. His routine stop on his way home after his late shifts for the past few weeks. When he stepped inside the apartment, he froze. The living room area lights illuminated the evening. The television flashed the evening news. He heard her soft voice.

"Thank you."

Pause.

"Yes."

Pause.

"I'm good."

Pause.

"I will."

A huge part of him sank with relief at the fact she was alive and safe. He braced himself on the doorknob and closed his eyes. His knees went weak. The combination of elation, fury, and burnout warred within him. He needed to let it out and the only person who deserved to hear his wrath finally returned.

He stepped further into the apartment, his blood pressure surging. He needed answers to his plentitude of questions and the time finally arrived to get them. Jason stood in the center of her apartment, his eyes scanning the room. Nothing out of place. No black bags or masks or diamonds laid out in the open. The obnoxious racket of the blender starting and stopping said she hadn't changed her diet. A protein drink. She hadn't been hurt. It hadn't been her. A slight twinge of doubt wanted to push forward.

But where the hell had she been for three weeks?

Jason listened to her fuss in the kitchen. She entered the room and stole his breath. Her beautiful features were pale and sunken, she wore her hair piled high in a loose bun. Black yoga pants and a white tee showed off her amazing figure. Barefoot, those black painted toenails peeked out from the hem of her pants.

His heart burst into a million relieved pieces. He wanted to hold her and know she was all right.

Hannah's eyes went wide as she stopped stiff. She muttered something under her breath he didn't catch.

Jason advanced on her and crashed his mouth into hers. He lifted her and carried her to the sofa, tumbling down with her, blanketing her with his big body. Furious, relieved, and frustrated, he poured all those emotions into the kiss, which could be described more like a battle between tongues than a show of affection. Hannah pulled at his shirt, her stubby nails raking down his back. Jason reached between them and yanked down her flimsy pants. He fumbled with his belt and his own pants. Their bodies gyrated frantically. A desperation to own her consumed Jason. To let her know she belonged to him. That whatever shit she got herself into would now stop. He was taking over.

Without any form of foreplay, Jason impaled her. She screamed and arched at the harsh invasion. He pounded into her thin body, his mouth never breaking from her as he worked his way down her jaw and neck, savoring the taste of her. He'd thought he would never see or touch her again. He'd never known pain as the thought of not having another night with her, of not being able to taste her delectable mouth or inhale her flowery scent. His hips hammered into her as he plowed deeper, wanting to crawl inside her body and own her. His hands raked over her soft skin, lifting her tee to expose her stomach. His body roughly consumed hers, searing himself into her skin. Hannah belonged to him and she needed to understand that the illegal lifestyle she lived ended pronto.

Without warning, she exploded around him, wailing out his name. Jason followed her, emptying himself into her body, filling her with his seed. His body sagged on top of hers. His head burrowing into the crook of her neck, trying to get air into his lungs.

Hannah's body trembled beneath his, barely audible sobs savagely cut straight to his heart.

Jason lifted his head, wrecked by her tear-streaked beautiful features.

"I'm sorry," she cried.

He kissed her gently on the lips. "We'll figure this out."

And they would. He couldn't lose her. Not to the law, not to a bullet, not to a life on the run. Whatever Jason needed to do, he would to keep her. At that moment, he chose the opposite path he'd been living his entire life.

## 38

Hannah's body soreness had begged for Jason to stop earlier, but her mind overruled the natural instinct to push him away. She understood he needed the connection, to know she was alive and well, and to lay claim to her.

After he'd first had sex with her, Jason had taken her to bed and laid her on her stomach. His gentle touch traced the closed up, healing bullet wound.

"Who took care of you?" He flipped her onto her back, his warm comforting hand resting on her stomach.

"A doctor that the man who I've done business with knows." She laced her fingers with his.

"Who do you work with?" He lightly skimmed this thumb back and forth over their intertwined hands.

She hesitated, unsure of what she could admit.

"Don't keep me in the dark any longer." His eyes pleaded.

"His name is Carl and he works for Derrick Murphy."

Jason blinked, his eyes widening. "Holy shit. Do you know who he is?"

"I do."

"Hannah, you're not just in deep. You're working with the most dangerous man in the Northeast."

"Who saved my life."

Jason stared at her, not uttering a word until he pushed her onto her stomach again to study her wound. "I suppose he did and I should be grateful."

He stroked her low back, the injury a bit tender to touch. "This hasn't completely healed. We need to get you to a regular doctor."

"I'll be fine."

"This is non-negotiable. Tomorrow, we'll get it examined." He kissed her wound and rested his cheek against her back as his arms wound around her tightly.

They hadn't spoken a word after but they'd made love two more times.

Three in the morning and she lay wide awake, fearful of what Jason would do. Would he arrest her and turn her in? As far as she understood, the police had no proof of her involvement in the heists. But what happened while she'd been gone for weeks, she remained clueless. And she refused to admit she was in fact the woman he and his fellow officers sought.

Jason's large arm currently wrapped protectively around her waist and his right leg clamped over hers. But she needed to take a Motrin. She trembled, more from a chill than anything else.

Squirming her way out of his hold, she plodded out of the bedroom to the kitchen. Hunched over the sink, she braced herself on the counter and held her back where that damn bullet pierced her body. Hannah thought she'd been doing well with her recovery, on the mend. But sex with Jason reminded her that her body had far more healing to do. She should have known better. She hated that her decision making skills lacked appropriate judgment.

She broke out in a cold sweat. Her stomach pitched, like she was going to—

Hannah's body convulsed as she vomited into the sink. Her body wrenched in pain as her stomach heaved.

"Hannah." Jason appeared behind her, grabbing her waist to hold her upright. "It's a greenish yellow. We need to get you to the hospital."

She shook her head. Medical staff would ask questions. There was no record of her anywhere being treated for a gunshot wound. Eventually the unanswered inquiries would lead her to a jail cell. She needed to call Carl.

"I won't allow anything to happen to you. But clearly you've got an infection. You need the hospital." His tone begged with a bite to it.

She opened her mouth to respond but collapsed into Jason's arms, the room spinning and the lights fading.

*** 

An annoying beep echoed throughout Hannah's dreams. Dreams that consisted of her and Jason lounging on a Hawaiian beach, watching the soft waves roll in, Hannah curled into his big body.

Beep.

Jason gently stroking her arm in a rhythmic motion. Lulling her asleep.

That fucking annoying beep again.

A soft kiss on her forehead. Peacefully watching the sun set in each other's arms.

Beep.

"Hannah." His voice distant, she tried to focus on him but his features began to drift off.

Beep.

"Hannah."

Her eyes fluttered and suddenly she was ripped from the serene ambiance of the tropical beach. Florescent lighting blinded her as her eyes tried to adjust and the scent of bleach stung her nose.

"Hey, baby," Jason said.

Her head flopped to the left. Jason's worn features looked at her with profound relief. He reached up and brushed her hair out of her eyes. "Thank God you're awake."

"What happened?" She winced at the pain that strangled her throat.

"You have an infection. You're on IV antibiotics," he said.

She went to move her right hand but cold steel pinched her wrist. She closed her eyes, pushing the rising panic down.

"You told them." She opened her eyes, her hurt probably spewing. She couldn't feel betrayed. She couldn't reasonably be angry or disappointed. None of those emotions would be fair to him.

"No," he said.

Another voice piped in. "We had all hospitals on alert for a woman with a gunshot wound to the back. Surprisingly it took three weeks for her to come in."

Jason's chief stood off to the right side of the room, along with Dean. Both men dressed in jeans and T-shirts. Dean looked sympathetically at her while the Chief looked downright pissed off.

"I'm under arrest?"

"Yes," Chief answered. "Rooney."

Dean reluctantly read her Miranda rights. Hannah ignored Dean. Tears spilled down her cheeks.

"I love you." She was overwrought with despair. "I never meant to fall in love with you, but I did. I didn't want to fall in love with you. But I have. Your warm smile makes my heart melt. I cherish the safety your strong arms wrapped around me at night give me. Your laugh makes me smile inside out. I love listening to you hum when you cook or when you're fixing your tie in the mornings. I love how you get all the answers wrong on every game show, but you continue to play along. I love how you watch me, like there's no one else in existence. I love how you whisper in my ear before we fall asleep and tell me how much you love me. I love that you love me. I love you, Jason."

She closed her eyes, her body shaking with barely contained sobs.

Dean had stopped his reciting her rights.

Except for the bothersome noise from the machines that fed her the appropriate medicine, nothing invaded her anguish.

If she never had contact with Jason again, she wanted him to know what was truly in her heart. That when she agreed to marry him, she did from her whole heart. That when she was with him, nothing else mattered except for him. That all those tiny things that most women might consider annoying, she loved.

Hannah opened her eyes to look into Jason's. Those striking blue eyes glistened as he blinked rapidly. He leaned over and kissed her on the lips.

"I love you." He leaned in, only the two of them existing, pushing out the invasion of the world into their bubble. She hated herself for what she'd done to him.

"Body and soul, I love you." He whispered into her ear, their conversation remaining between the two of them. "I'll do whatever it takes to get you out of this."

"Don't. I did this on my own. I knew the consequences. Don't risk your career for me," she said.

"I don't have a choice. I'll risk anything for you. I cannot go another day without you by my side. I've lived in hell for the last three weeks, thinking you could possibly be dead. I won't go through that torture again." He took her hand and kissed the engagement ring on her finger. He placed her hand over his heart in a silent promise.

## 39

Jason held the resignation letter in his hands and inspected it for the tenth time.

"I know what you're thinking." Chief sidled up to Jason's desk. "Don't do it."

He glanced up at his boss. Why the hell wouldn't he resign? "There's too much shit about to come down on you. The press will get hold of the fact that I've been dating and sleeping with the jewelry thief we've been after for over two years. This entire precinct, including you, will look like clowns."

"And you'll have to testify against her." Chief sat down on the edge of his desk.

"That'll never happen." He planned on marrying Hannah quickly to take care of that hurdle. He wouldn't have to testify against his own wife. This plan laid contingent on her release from the hospital. The infection that poisoned her body took its toll. She should have been treated by medical professionals in a facility. Another righteous browbeating he planned to have with her.

"The hell it won't." Chief's face turned red. It was almost comical. "You're a cop. You took an oath."

"Fuck the oath." He stood, ready to go toe-to-toe with his boss. The man didn't get it. Chief's job ruled his life. He had no one else. The man's career was his wife. He had tunnel vision when it came to the law. No veering off the road. Everyone had to walk a straight line or else receive the infamous tirade Chief projected. Chief didn't understand what it meant to find someone who could own his heart. A woman who he'd gladly hand it over to and would die trying to protect. A partner who filled the cavernous hole in his soul.

"My primary concern is Hannah. She comes first, above everything."

"Including your brothers?"

"Including my brothers. But I know they'll have my back no matter my decision, because I'd have theirs." Jason shoved his letter at his boss. "Consider this my last day."

"Consider this your last minute. Get the hell out of my unit." Chief stood, snatched the letter out of his hand. "You're making a mistake putting your career on the line for a woman who's going to do a great deal of time in prison. And all you're going to do is end up spending time behind bars yourself if you don't cooperate. Jail isn't a friendly place to an officer, even a former one."

Chief spun and headed toward his office but stopped and fixated on the entry door. Jason watched one of the most notorious attorneys in the city walk into the precinct. Dan Turner, a terrific defense attorney and considered the bane of their existence, headed straight for their chief. Only the wealthy could afford Mr. Turner's services. Who did they arrest that had the man stepping foot into their building?

"Chief Reynolds." Turner beamed, holding out a hand. "What a pleasure. It's been too long."

His now *former* boss crossed his arms over his chest, ignoring the proffered friendly greeting. "To what do I owe the non-pleasure, Mr. Turner?"

"Why don't we speak in private." It was not a suggestion by the attorney.

Every officer on duty stopped in middle of their errands, engrossed in the scene.

"Nick, who did they arrest last night?" Jason asked as Chief and Dan waltzed into the office and closed the door behind them.

"No one," Nick said.

Jordan, the new detective brought on to temporarily replace Tyler, whistled. "Dan Turner doesn't randomly show up at police stations for our every day arrests. Someone with deep pockets hired that man."

Dean approached Jason, empty box in hand. "I think you're making a mistake."

"I'm not."

"What are you going to do?" his longtime partner and best friend asked.

Jason took the box and started to toss what few personal items he had inside. He didn't keep much in or on his desk. He worked simplistically. He scooped up the picture of him and Hannah in front of the fountain at The Point. Reasonably, Jason understood he should be livid he had a picture of her on his desk for months and the entire time she'd been living a dangerous, illegal secret life. But he didn't have it in him to hate her or hold a grudge. Hannah was his life. With her in his arms, he was whole. Alive. She gave him someone and something to come home to nightly. Yes, she still had questions to answer, but he had an inkling of the element to her crime spree. Her parents. Deep down he knew they were somehow involved.

"I don't know." Truthfully he didn't have a plan. At the moment, Hannah's health and freedom was priority number one. "But I have a bit of money saved. I'll figure it out."

"Jason–"

They were interrupted by the door to Chief's office flying open and Dan Turner sauntering out of the building. Chief's angry form took up the frame. He drilled Jason with a glare.

"So your girl hired the best attorney in the area. Wonder where she got the money to flip his bill?" Chief slammed the door shut so hard, the glass shattered, shards raining down onto the floor. Dean and Nick rushed into their boss's office.

Jason ignored the tantrum. He had something more important in his life now to focus on, and find out how she managed to hire Attorney Turner.

## 40

"Carl, I can't thank you enough." Hannah hugged the portly man. Turned out she should have gone to Carl a long time ago. A decision she would forever regret not making by virtue of her extensive list of *what ifs*.

She turned to her high-powered attorney Dan Turner, outside of the courtroom. "Thank you."

"You're quite welcome. Without a spent bullet removed from your body by a hospital for ballistics to match Officer O'Neill's service weapon, they have no evidence against you and will drop the case. It'll go cold. The feds, who don't have a case either, have come into their building and are now doing their own internal investigation. That precinct will be under scrutiny for a while." Mr. Turner bent down and spoke quietly, for the two of them. "I suggest you find a new career."

Hannah nodded. "I plan to, with my husband."

She faced Mr. Murphy, who had hired her attorney to keep her out of jail—for selfish reasons on his part. All her activities eventually may have led back to him. Not that she would have ever turned on Carl. She would have gone to her grave hiding the fact he took her stolen diamonds. But with their appearances by her side, it didn't take a genius to figure out where the jewels had disappeared to. "I owe you."

The handsome man grinned, pure malevolence exuding from him. "Be careful what you verbally put out in the universe. I tend to collect. Right now, I've decided we're even. The large amount of money earned off your little crime spree has pleased me. Anything else I have to do for you, you *will* owe me."

She saluted him. "Yes, sir."

The man chuckled. "Why couldn't my wife have your reasonable personality?"

Hannah laughed. "Reasonable? I lied to my fiancé, who happened to be a detective working the case to catch me. I dated him, stupidly fell in love, and even worse agreed to marry him. I'm probably far more trouble than your wife could ever be."

He cocked a brow. "You do not know my wife. But you are absolutely correct. I will never introduce the two of you. Who knows what schemes you would both cook up?"

Mr. Murphy placed a gentle hand on her shoulder. "Take care of yourself. If you do need anything, you call me."

"I will," she said. "Thank you, again."

She watched all three men saunter off with an outrageous entourage. The scene quite ludicrous. All three men clearly knew each other well and their camaraderie evident by their upbeat male banter as they left the building. All eyes focused on the group as they exited.

Guilt was an emotion Hannah learned to rid herself of years ago. A necessity for her survival skills to develop. But when she turned to find Jason leaning against a far wall, intently watching the scene, that damn nagging conscience crept into her psyche. A voice that questioned whether or not Jason might ever trust her, now that her legal issues had vanished.

Jason pushed off the wall and approached. His large arm encircled her waist. "Let's go home. We finally need to have a discussion. We've put it off far too long."

Jason led her out to his car, her hand placed securely in his. As they passed his former LEO brothers, Nick called out to him. "Jason."

He kept leading her away, perfectly content with not speaking to any of his former brothers.

"Jason, you should talk to them." She'd driven a wedge between him and the friends he'd known for years. Men he'd been through hell and back with. She didn't want that for him.

"Jason." Dean skidded in front of them. "Buddy, stop."

Nick came up next to Dean. "Congratulations, Hannah."

She didn't respond. What could she say, *thanks*?

"Just because you're not on the force doesn't mean we're enemies," Dean said.

"You want to put my fiancée in jail."

Nick shrugged negligently. "We have bigger issues at the moment and have not one bit of evidence of wrongdoing, as brought up in court by her excellent attorney."

Dean slapped a hand on Jason's shoulder. "Listen, we only want what's best for you. If you believe Hannah is where you want your future, we'll support that decision. If leaving the force has to be part of that, well, I'm not too keen on the idea, but it's your life. You've stood by both of our sides when we've gone through hell. I can't easily turn my back on that loyalty, man. It's the least I owe you."

"What he said." Nick pointed to Dean.

Hannah nudged Jason when he didn't respond. "Jason, don't use me as a crutch to push away your best friends."

Jason stared his brothers down. "She's off limits."

"As long as she finds a better nighttime job and doesn't force our hand." Dean pointed to Chief and Tyler, on crutches, behind them, glaring their direction. "Those two will hold onto their animosity until they keel over."

Hannah watched Jason internally wrestle with how to accept this outreach from his friends. When he finally nodded, they all breathed out a sigh of relief.

"Thanks." He took part in a manly hug from both friends. "I'm taking Hannah home. She's still not a hundred percent."

Nick flashed Hannah a stern frown. "Stay out of trouble. If you instigate any more problems, I'll be the one to come after you."

Hannah smiled and batted her lashes. "If I ever give Jason a difficult time, I would hope you would have his back."

Jason quickly ushered her into his car before they all got into a pissing contest.

On their way home, Hannah stared out the car window, oblivious to the beautiful fall scenery passing by. Her mind battled with doubt after the conversation with Dean and Nick. How could Jason forgive her for what she put him through? How could she keep herself from falling into the trap of wanting to protect herself and run? Already she concerned herself with hiding cash. Last night she slept restlessly, a nightmare about men in suits hunting her, but she had no money on hand to get out of town. She woke in a cold sweat and ended up on the sofa at three in the morning, watching horrible reality show repeats.

Jason gently picked up her left hand and kissed the diamond. Two weeks since she'd returned and they hadn't been able to find their footing. It didn't help that jail time had weighed heavily on them. Now that they no longer needed to worry about Hannah behind bars, they needed to figure out how to move forward.

"I never meant to lie to you." She broke the chafing silence.

"Really?" She heard the doubt in his tone.

What a stupid comment. "All right, I did mean to lie to you. But I never meant to fall in love with you. I wasn't purposely playing a game with your emotions. I never meant for it to go as far as it did. After our first date, I wanted to turn you down, remember? But you relentlessly pursued. And I didn't have it in me to say no. I loved being with you."

He didn't say anything, just let go of her hand and tightened his grip on the steering wheel.

"I admit, I had thought about using you at first. But Roy talked me out of it. And after thinking about his advice, he was right. I'm not the type of person to use the people around me. That's my parents. I've done everything in my power to make certain I don't repeat their pattern. But I failed, and I allowed them to continue to affect me, all the while convincing myself that I wasn't making the same mistakes. That I'd gotten over the life I'd been given as a child and young girl." Her conversation with Jason over dinner and how she vehemently expressed how her parents didn't influence her came to mind.

A slight twinge of regret jolted through her. Last week, Carl showed up on her doorstep with a newspaper clipping. He didn't say a word as he handed her the article, turned and walked back to a waiting black SUV. The front page article, with a picture of her parents, reported the death of a husband and wife, their lifeless bodies found in a stolen vehicle in Canada, not far from the US border. At the time, she slid to the floor, her heart broken for what she never had—parents who didn't put themselves in a position to be murdered in a car they stole. Jason had rushed into the room and held her as she sat on the hardwood floor for the longest time, weeping.

"Why did you start?" he asked.

She couldn't face him, the heat of shame climbing up her neck. But she owed him an explanation and answers to any and all questions. She had to push through, no matter how uncomfortable the subject. "I needed the money quickly. I had nothing. I was an eighteen-year-old high school dropout who just had her legs broken by men her parents screwed over. They thought hurting me would get my parents to pay up. They underestimated my parents' need for drugs more than the willingness to protect their only child. As soon as I could, I left and found myself holed up in a seedy hotel in Erie with a hundred dollars to my name. Money earned from working at a fast food restaurant back home. I was desperate and seconds away from living on streets I didn't know how to survive.

"The first place I robbed was a pawn shop located in the shittiest part of the city. It was too easy. I managed to make a thousand dollars and knew I found a quick way to make cash. I spent the next eight years on the run. Staying in a town for a year or so at the most. The last time my parents' debt caught up to me, the men stating that I never fully paid, I ended up with broken legs again. I got a bus ticket to Pittsburgh. That's when I found Roy, who was having a panic attack in middle of a grocery store. I was picking up Motrin and barely making it around on crutches." She wiped a stray tear she hadn't realized escaped. "I helped him out to my car and offered him a ride home. He offered me a place to stay."

She remembered the painful time in her life.

"Roy catered to me even back then. Despite the fact he has issues, his loyalty and caring is something I'll forever cherish and be grateful for. Sleeping on Roy's sofa was the first time in my life I could safely rest. After I recovered, I disappeared off the radar, certain I couldn't be tracked. I've paid in cash for everything, changed my hair from brown to red, and developed a new wardrobe style. I've kept my head down, away from surveillance cameras that a knowledgeable PI might be able to identify me from. My real name is Cynthia Raymond. Roy came up with Hannah Lakely." She'd referred to it as her stripper name when he'd first presented her with her license and fake birth certificate.

"I like Hannah better." Jason's knuckles were white as he gripped the wheel harder.

"So do I," she said. "Lakely is a bit much. Roy thought the name was hysterical. He says it resembled a bad porn name and is too over-the-top."

"Are you going to introduce me to him?"

"Do you want to meet him?"

"Yes." There was no hesitation to his answer.

"All right."

"Why, after you paid the money, did you continue?" Ah, leave it to her detective fiancé to mine deeper.

"I convinced myself those men would return. Honestly, I was greedy, using my parents as convenient scapegoats to latch on to. It was nice having money, a clean bed to sleep in. Food in the pantry. Living in crime free neighborhoods. Having a safe home without drug paraphernalia littering every surface." The warm tears flowed down her cheeks. "I don't know any other way to support myself."

Jason remained silent while she used the edge of her light jacket to wipe her tears.

He pulled the car into his garage and they meandered into his home. It hadn't yet turned into *their* home. A gaping disconnect remained between them, as if waiting for the other shoe to drop. All her fault. No one else could take the blame.

He set his keys on the gray marble top of the kitchen island and leaned forward, his hands bracing himself. His head hung, deep lines around his eyes evidence his weariness wore him down.

Hannah slid up next to him and laid her head on his bicep. "I'm so sorry. For everything."

Jason wrapped his right arm around her and pulled her into his body. She allowed his warmth to surround and embrace her. She relished his love and devotion. Despite everything she'd done to him, he managed to find the strength to stick by her.

"I need you," Jason said. "I don't want to live a life without you. But I have no idea how to go about moving forward or past this. I have no idea what we do from here."

Her heart ached. "I know."

She gazed up at him, studying his handsome features. She could spend hours just staring at him and never grow tired. "I can only promise you that I'm going to work every day to prove to you that we're going to be okay. I need you in my life, too. This isn't the way a relationship should start. But I honestly believe fate brought us together. I love you."

Jason leaned down and kissed her, his lips gently caressing hers. She returned his kiss with passion, expressing how much he meant to her. How much she loved him. How much she was devoted to him.

"Marry me." Jason wrenched away from their lip lock.

"You've already asked and I've already said yes."

"We need to get this done ASAP. But a real ceremony with vows and promises and all that other stuff that means more than some magistrate reciting legal jargon." Which had been their original plan.

Hannah pulled back. "Legal jargon? This coming from a man of the law."

"Former. And I need you to help me open up a PI office. We can be partners. Your skills for getting in and out of places could come in handy. We'll be partners, you can take classes for the business, giving you skills to learn how to support us, yourself." Jason lovingly pulled her hair aside and planted a kiss on the side of her neck. "My mother will be ecstatic as soon as I tell her that we're getting married."

"You haven't told her yet?"

He kissed her forehead. "I haven't told them anything. There'd be too many questions and I don't want my father to treat you differently. He'd disapprove. There are some things that would be better left in the dark. This is a major one."

"If that's how you want to handle this. I'll follow your lead." He protected her at all costs, even from the potential backlash of his family if they discovered the truth.

He grinned devilishly and nuzzled her neck, his hands roaming under her shirt. "Just keep saying those words and all will be good."

"Oh no." She pushed out of his fondling. "You will not use this as a weapon against me for the rest of our lives."

"Don't intend to, babe." Jason pulled her back into his body. "I just need to keep a close eye on you from here on out."

"I think we could arrange something small, here at the house." She changed the subject.

"Good." He nipped her earlobe.

"And I happen to know someone who can help get the PI business up and running, especially the technical side of things." Hannah toyed with the buttons on his light blue shirt.

"Roy?" Jason guessed.

She nodded.

"He helped you, didn't he?"

She nodded again.

Jason's head fell back on his shoulders. "You two are going to be the death of me, aren't you?"

Hannah grimaced. "We are not. And speaking of being the death of you. I have a huge favor to ask."

"Okay?"

"Can we move Roy into the house?"

"What?" His voice went up an octave, pushing back from her. "Why the hell would you ask that?"

"He's my best friend. He's watched out for me for years. And he's alone in an apartment, unable to really take care of himself, paralyzed by his gripping fear. In our house he'll be around people he trusts. He'll have more than three rooms to live in and better conditions. He'll have a family. Us." Hannah pulled her hair back into a ponytail, ready for a battle.

"He's like my brother, Jason. I've explained to you about my family and what that means. When I say that Roy is my family, along with you and your parents, that means everything to me." She sat on one of the stools, her back hunching. "I had no one until Roy came into my life. If we hadn't bumped into each other, I would most certainly be dead by now."

Jason studied her, his mouth opening and closing a couple times, as if going to argue but thinking better of it. He visibly sagged. "Let me meet him first."

It was all she could really ask for. If Jason turned down her request, she'd just have to make the twenty mile trip into the city a couple times a week.

"Thank you." She popped up on her toes and kissed him.

He cocked a brow. "I could use a better show of appreciation than that."

"Really?" She lifted her shirt over her head and shimmied out of her bra, exposing herself. "What do you have in mind?"

Jason picked her up, laid her on the island, and feasted upon her, losing himself in her.

Hannah was home. Jason was her lifeline, her beating heart, her soul. She'd do anything necessary to hold onto the meaningful life he vowed to give her and in return, give Jason all of her without conditions or fear of ever losing her.

# Epilogue

Jason's backyard had been transformed into a wedding celebration—white lights and canopies, a hardwood dance floor, a DJ, and a group of about fifty people in full party mode. When Jason and Hannah found out the late November day would be in the low seventies, they quickly changed the event from indoors to outside. Thank goodness these people weren't crammed into his home.

He held a beer in one hand, leaning against a porch pillar, watching his beautiful wife dance with his father, who admitted to being smitten with his daughter-in-law.

"She's stunning." His mother approached from exiting the back of the house.

Jason lifted his arm and wrapped his mom up in a snug embrace. "She is."

"I'm so happy for you."

"Thanks, Mom. Hannah makes me happy." He took a swig of his beer. His parents remained clueless over Hannah's brush with the law. The media took interest in the case but didn't have enough information to make assumptions. The reporters focused mainly on the feds involvement and the lack of oversight within the police department. Hannah's contact and attorney managed to keep her name out of the news. Her connections confounded him.

His dad asked a couple questions but didn't delve deeply. Jason would go to his grave before he told his mother and father about her former life. His dad wouldn't understand. His mother, despite being a saint, would consider Hannah not a good fit to be an officer's wife. Not that he owned a badge any longer. But his mom would forever consider him a man of the law.

"I see Dean and Nick are here, but Tyler and Chief refused your invitations." His mother's unasked question was not well disguised.

"Tyler's still hampered by his leg, Mom." Not entirely true. According to Dean, Tyler's rehab had him on the rebound quicker than expected. His tenacious personality paying off with regard to getting himself out of a cast and off crutches. Tyler refused the invite. His former LEO brother, no matter who told him to let the case go, wouldn't and held a resentment against Jason and his newlywed wife. He couldn't blame Tyler for hating Hannah. But Tyler did shoot Hannah and Jason didn't hold onto ill well for that mistake. Tyler needed to take the same mindset, but the kid couldn't be forced. He would have to accept the team's failure on this case in due time.

"I heard he's doing well. That Kayla moved in with him," his mom said.

"Yep."

"But I'm a bit offended by your former chief not showing up."

"Mom, his precinct is under investigation right now and I didn't exactly leave on a solid note. He's pissed. He'll get over it someday." Jason didn't expect that to truly occur. He grappled with a sense of loss over his chief ending their friendship, but understood why.

"Are you sure you want to open a PI office?" she asked for the hundredth time. Each time she questioned him, he only stated that he couldn't do the job of an officer any more. That he feared his safety for Hannah's sake.

His father, on the other hand, became ecstatic when he found out Jason planned to become a private investigator. His dad jumped on board immediately, offering his services. Jason had every intention on taking the old man up on that offer.

"I am."

"Good." His mom patted his chest. "I'll finally be able to sleep at night. I haven't done that in over thirty years."

Jason leaned down and kissed the top of her head. He loved his mother dearly and now got to share that love with Hannah.

Dean and Nick approached, Dean with his parents' neighbor's daughter under arm and Nick nursing a glass of red wine.

"Dean." His mother's smile turned downward. "Aren't you a little old for Britney? She's only twenty-one."

Dean jerked away from the young woman as if he'd been bit by a snake. Nick snorted. Jason chuckled and shook his head.

"You told me you were twenty-eight."

The girl shrugged. Dean rolled his eyes. "Yeah, no. Sorry."

"Thanks a lot Mrs. Campbell." The girl stomped off, pouting.

"Nice." Jason titled his beer in a mock salute.

"I'll go talk to her parents about this little incident. That girl should not be going around lying about her age." His mom rushed off, indignant.

Nick slapped Jason on the back. "Congratulations. I hope this works out for you, man."

"It will." Jason wouldn't allow any other outcome.

He watched Hannah and his father end their dance, laughing together, her beautiful eyes bright and happy.

"Who's the guy in the house?" Dean nodded to the second floor window.

Jason didn't bother to glance up. "Roy."

"Who's Roy?" Nick's attention focused upward, behind them.

"Hannah's best friend." He finished off his beer while he watched his wife search the crowd. When she locked eyes on him, her grin turned to a wide smile. She walked over to the gift table and picked up a small box, wrapped in white paper, and headed his direction.

"Why won't he come outside?" Dean asked. "It's weird."

Jason punched his friend in the arm. "He's agoraphobic, ass."

"Jesus." Dean rubbed his arm. "I can't imagine."

"Yeah, the move was pretty rough. But Hannah knows how to handle him." Jason had watched the two carefully when they emptied Roy's apartment and moved him into one of the spare bedrooms in his home. Their interaction reminded him of siblings with the way they argued and the manner in which Hannah catered to Roy and vice versa. At first, Jason had been concerned about intimacy between the two, but after seeing their banter first hand, he relaxed. No way would those two ever cross that line. In fact, when he suggested it, only in passing once, Hannah rushed to the bathroom and vomited.

"Isn't it odd having him in your home?" Taking a sip of his wine, Nick zeroed in on where Dean pointed.

"Not at all. He's usually up all night and sleeps during the day. Some days we don't even see him unless Hannah checks on him. We're both starting to nag him to come out of his room to join us for dinner or a movie. He's starting to warm up to his environment. My mom loves him. She's all over him like a newborn child. My dad's fascinated by his computer knowledge and visits to quiz him on purchasing a new PC."

"What does he do for income?" Dean snatched a beer out of a passing waiter's hand.

"He's got mad computer skills. He creates programs for companies based off their needs. He does a lot of odd jobs, too. He works with missing persons charities." Jason found out through casual conversation with Roy that charity work meant the world to him. Apparently his medical condition triggered after being traumatized from an abduction of a foster child out of a home he stayed in as a teen.

Jason pitied Roy. Early this morning, Roy's distress over not being able to even step into the backyard to watch their wedding ceremony almost spurred a break down. Jason intervened and assured Roy that from his bedroom window, he'd be able to see and hear everything perfectly. They planned that part of the celebration specifically with Roy in mind.

Roy had calmed down and profusely thanked him. "Thank you Jason, for everything. I know it must have been difficult agreeing to take me in. But thank you. Hannah's the only family I have."

Jason responded with a rebuke. "That's not true. You're my family. Therefore, my family, my parents, uncles, and cousins are now your family, too."

After that, Roy asked for some time alone. Jason supposed he needed a moment to compose himself from overwhelming gratitude.

"Really?" Dean quizzically observed Roy, who opened the window and had a plate of food in hand.

"Yeah."

Hannah approached him and handed him the gift she held. "Happy wedding day."

He chuckled. "Didn't know we were getting each other gifts."

"Yeah, I should have mentioned that." Those large eyes sparkled mischievously.

Dean and Nick each barked out a laugh.

"'Atta girl. You keep him on his toes." Dean winked.

Hannah smiled bashfully, a full out acting job. "I would never do that to my husband."

"Said the jewelry thief," Nick said out of the corner of his mouth to Dean.

Jason tossed him a glare while Hannah flipped him off.

He unwrapped the rectangle box and lifted the lid. Inside was a white and purple stick with a window. Inside the window was two pink lines.

"Oh shit," Nick said.

"What is this?" Jason asked.

"A pregnancy test."

"What?" His head jerked up.

"Remember when you came to my apartment? I was sick and on an antibiotic. I'd also had IV antibiotics in the hospital."

He nodded, his mouth slack. Nick reached over and pushed closed his hanging jaw.

"They diluted my birth control. I'm ten weeks pregnant."

Jason's mind reeled. He lost his breath. His heart thrummed so hard he thought it would beat right out of his chest. His Hannah, pregnant. With his baby. His eyes bounced to her flat stomach and back up and back down. His hands automatically went to her belly.

"Hannah."

"I love you."

"Oh my God, I love you." Jason took her mouth in a blazing kiss. The wedding attendees whooped and hollered, unaware of the news, thinking the bride and groom gifted them with a show of love.

Jason broke the kiss and held her beautiful face in his hands. He loved her with every ounce of his being. She opened up his heart and took hold of it for herself. He gladly handed it to her. Hell, he'd serve it on a platter if she wanted. Hannah had made him happier than he ever thought he could experience when he met her. Now that she became his wife, Jason sealed his fate with hers. Soon they would be parents. Together. A piece of Jason and a piece of Hannah in one tiny human.

Jason scooped her up into his arms and carried her into the house and up the stairs to their bedroom.

"Jason," she protested. "We can't consummate our marriage right now."

"The hell we can't, baby. They'll be waiting for us when we return."

"*If* we return." Hannah's eyes glittered.

"Exactly. I'm just going to remind you how this baby came to be." He kicked the bedroom door closed behind them and swung her onto their bed. Jason shrugged out of his black tuxedo jacket.

He crooked his finger. "Let me strip you out of that dress. I have to spend some time worshiping my girl."

Jason would spend the rest of his life doing just that and whatever else it took to show his adoration for his Hannah.

\*\*\*

When Dean Rooney thought his soul couldn't be destroyed any more than it already had been, his best friend's wife announced her pregnancy. Dean took a shot of Jamison.

"Are you all right?" Nick asked.

"Perfectly fine." A lie. His son would have been five-years-old by now. He could envision his beautiful Erin standing by his side, utterly happy for Jason and Hannah. Their son running around with the other children, enjoying the party.

"Liar." Nick called him out on his shit.

Dean shrugged. His cell phone rang, saving him from Nick's delve into his suffering. He answered without looking at the caller ID.

Chief didn't wait for Dean to greet the call. "We need you at 500 Lock Lane. A woman has been attacked in her home. They have the guy in cuffs, but he's saying it's mistaken identity."

"Where's the woman?"

"Hospital, in surgery," Chief said.

"I've been drinking."

"Is Nick with you?"

"Yes."

"Has he been drinking?"

"A glass of wine." Dean mouthed *Chief* to his newly assigned partner.

"He'll lead." Chief hung up.

Dean shoved the phone back into his jacket pocket. "Duty calls."

"Are you serious?"

"Yeah, and you're leading this one." Dean lobbed Nick his car keys, thankful for the excuse of an early exit. He couldn't handle staying another minute with the happy couple, now with a child on the way. A nightmare reminder of what he'd lost five years ago.

"What do we have?" Nick asked as they left without proper farewells.

"A brutal assault." Dean hoped to hell the woman survived whatever had her in surgery.

###

## A Note From the Author

I would like to personally thank you for making Heist a part of your library. In today's saturated market of romance novels and limited time we have for reading, I'm honored you chose Heist, Jason and Hannah. If you've enjoyed their story, I would be grateful if you left a small review, a necessity for *all* authors in today's industry.

I look forward to bringing you more from The Men of Law series and taking you on their journey, as well as introducing you to the women who bring these men to their knees.

Keep up-to-date on the shenanigans your favorite characters are stirring up by visiting www.CaseyClipper.com.

Again, thank you and happy reading!

~Casey

## About the Author

Contemporary Romance Author Casey Clipper lives in Pittsburgh, PA. She is a noted sports lover, chocolate addict, and has a slight obsession with penguins. Like you, she loves to lose herself in a good romance book. Casey is a PAN member of the Romance Writers of America, and an active member of the Three Rivers Romance Writers, Contemporary Romance Writers, Passionate Ink, ASMSG, and IAN.

Find out more about Casey's upcoming releases, appearances/signings, and freebie short story section by visiting www.CaseyClipper.com. Sign up for her newsletter, where she'll keep you up-to-date monthly on what's happening with her and around the romance world.

# Acknowledgements

The Killion Group, specifically Jenn and Jenn, who both keep me on task and feedback. They don't hold punches when it comes to my manuscripts. If you're looking for an editor who will give you honest opinions, I would suggest this group.

The fantastic Casey Clipper ebook and paperback covers are made by the terrific Joanna at Book Cover Master Class. I'm floored that each time we work together, it gets easier and easier because she understands what I love in a cover. I'm so glad to have her as part of the team.

Lieutenant Roger Wilson of the Ligonier Police Department, who kindly answered my questions. Not only was he easily approachable, he got back to me quickly and honestly with his answers to my odd questions. Roger, thank you for all you do for the community and for being an all around great guy.

If you're an author who is getting started on your own law enforcement novel, I would suggest picking up a novel that has great information on the different duties of different law enforcement agencies. M.A. Taylor's From a Cop's Viewpoint: Investigations 101 is a great resource. Not only is the text witty, she goes into great detail for each department in law enforcement. I've taken her workshops at the Romance Writers of America national conference every year for the past three years and learn something new every time. There are many different resources out there to help.

Heist wouldn't be here if it wasn't for my beta team, whose honesty I value. I thank you ladies for your time and terrific feedback and your amazing loyalty.

Clipp's Crew Street Team are a group of women who are my biggest cheerleaders. I love them and am entirely grateful for the hard work and dedication they have toward getting the word out about my novels. Their tireless work never goes unnoticed or unappreciated. Thank you ladies!

Book bloggers and pages that have shown such amazing support for my novels. I can't thank them enough for posting releases, sales, having contests, events, all the work they do to show their love for romance novels. Your dedication and love is never lost on me or my team. Thank you for all you do.

The Romance Writers of America and the Three Rivers Romance Writers. The Romance Writers of America has opened so many doors I had no idea existed. The national conference each year is an eye opening experience and always come as just the right time, when I'm personally in need of a recharge. The number of authors I've met through the RWA is astounding and am grateful for this organizations work toward the romance industry. The Three Rivers Romance Writers is a wonderful group of romance writers and authors and am honored to have become good friends with a few of these supportive women.

And last but definitely not least, you, the reader and lover of romance novels. I cannot begin to express how much I appreciate your support of not only my novels but the romance industry in general. Your devotion to the romance genre is unrivaled. Thank you for reading, falling in love with romance, with book boyfriends, and falling in love with your favorite romance authors.

Casey Clipper Novels Currently Available

**The Men of Law**
Heist (Book 1)
TBD (Book 2, beginning of 2016)
TBD (Book 3, July 2016)
TBD (Book 4, November 2016)

**The Love Series**
Silent Love (Book 1)
Unexpected Love (Book 2)
Dangerous Love (Book 3)
Taken Love (Book 4, the final installment)

**A Quinn Brothers Story**
Fire (Story 1)
Snow (Story 2)
Ice (Coming December 2015)
Wind (Coming 2016)
Rain (Coming 2016)

**The Boss's Love**
The Boss's Love
Darren's Story: A Prequel to The Boss's Love
Courtney's Story: A Prequel to The Boss's Love
Derrick's Story: A Prequel to The Boss's Love

**Standalones**
Scarred (a novella)

# Follow Casey

Website: www.CaseyClipper.com
Facebook Author Page: Casey Clipper Author
Twitter: @cclipper2
BookBub Author Page
Instagram: CaseyClipper
Pinterest: Casey Clipper
Goodreads
Contact: c_clipper2@hotmail.com

Sign up for Casey Clipper's newsletter to get insider information on new and upcoming releases, future projects, newsletter contests, and much more by going to www.CaseyClipper.com.

Made in the USA
Columbia, SC
20 February 2018